CLAWS

RUSSELL JAMES

SEVERED PRESS
HOBART TASMANIA

CLAWS

Copyright © 2019 Russell James
Copyright © 2019 by Severed Press

WWW.SEVEREDPRESS.COM

ISBN: 978-1-925840-75-9

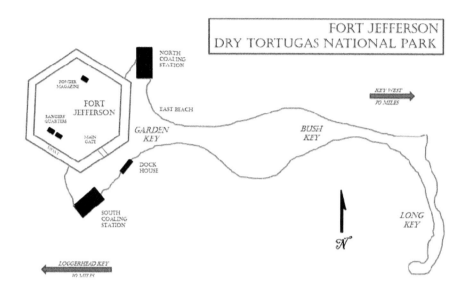

FORT JEFFERSON
DRY TORTUGAS NATIONAL PARK

POWDER
MAGAZINE

FORT
JEFFERSON

RANGERS
QUARTERS

MAIN
GATE

MOAT

NORTH
COALING
STATION

EAST BEACH

GARDEN
KEY

DOCK
HOUSE

SOUTH
COALING
STATION

BUSH
KEY

KEY WEST
70 MILES

LONG
KEY

𝒩

LOGGERHEAD KEY
70 MILES

Other titles by Russell James:

Professor Grant Coleman Series

Cavern of the Damned
Monsters in the Clouds
Curse of the Viper King

For Christy,

Who survived the tiny crabs during our Fort Jefferson adventure.

CHAPTER 1

Gianna Madera knew she'd never get out of this alive.

The cramped aft compartment of the ship stank of ancient sweat and stale seawater. If she hadn't disabled the enormous diesel engine beside her, the noise and heat would have degraded the atmosphere from miserable to unlivable. She knelt and clamped a small silver tube to one of the trawler's propeller shafts. A green light at one end of the sonic charge glowed.

Someone pulled at the bulkhead door from the other side. The rope she'd tied around the handle stretched tight, but held.

"She's in here!" a woman shouted.

Footsteps pounded against the deck. Whispers conspired in the passageway.

"Gianna!" the captain called. "It's a little late in the game to cause all this trouble. The work is done."

"But I can make sure it never gets ashore," Gianna said.

"No you can't. Listen."

She did. Rotor blades whined from somewhere above the upper deck.

"That's a helicopter I radioed to come pick up the emitters. They're already gone, off to do good work."

"I doubt that. If they were going to do *good* work, you wouldn't have kidnapped me and forced me to make them."

"That was about expediency," the captain said. "Sometimes timelines get compressed, and we have to cut corners. But as I've always said, you'll be well compensated. Since we're finished, we'll forget about this little incident, and you're free to go home on this chopper if you want. And we've explained your absence to your employer. You'll have no problems."

Gianna worked in a black ops section of Silenius Imports. The people on this boat had the combination of magnificent minds and missing morals that made them prime candidates to have connections there. But if this crew had legitimate government sponsorship, they wouldn't have had to resort to kidnapping, and would have been forthcoming about the ultimate plan for the sonic emitters she'd been forced to perfect.

Everything the captain spouted had to be a pack of lies.

"Forget it!" Giana shouted.

"Then you'll never get off this boat alive."

"Neither will any of you," she said to herself. "And neither will the emitters."

With a small screwdriver, she flipped a microswitch on the sonic charge attached to the propeller shaft. A green light turned red. The cylinder began to hum. Gianna scrambled to the other side of the big engine and ducked.

The charge spooled up and emitted an escalating, high-pitched scream. The driveshaft began to flex back and forth, as if the steel had turned to rubber. It clanged against the mounts at either end. The people in the passageway shouted in confusion.

The charge frequency peaked at a painful shriek. Giana covered her ears, but the noise seemed to penetrate straight through her skull.

The mounts sheared. The driveshaft ripped clear of the hull and tore a gaping hole in the transom. Water rushed in and swept the sonic charge into the sea before it could do more damage. The stern angled down. On the other side of the door, the passageway filled with the sounds of people scrambling away for the upper decks.

Gianna splashed through the rising water to the bulkhead door. She tried to untie the rope, but the others yanking at the door had cinched the knot tight. Water pooled around her calves. Her wet fingers slipped against the hard, nylon line.

"Damn it." She gave the rope a frustrated pull. The nobility of sacrificing herself to stop this unknown evil suddenly did not outweigh self-preservation.

A brainstorm struck. She pulled the tiny screwdriver from her pocket and wedged the tip into the heart of the knot. She wiggled and wiggled until the knot began to work free. Cold sea water lapped at her knees and her pulse throbbed so hard it made her hands shake. The boat angled further down.

The knot broke loose. She whipped the rope free of the door and tried to push the door open. With the boat angled back, the door seemed to weigh a ton. Her feet slipped on the submerged steel deck.

She took a deep breath, dug in, and heaved. The door slowly rose, then past the halfway point, then slammed down on the other side as gravity started to work for instead of against her. Water surged out of the engine room and into the empty corridor.

From the deck overhead came the splash of a launching lifeboat and the shouts of the panicked crew.

For the first time since she'd entered the engine room with the sonic charge, Gianna dared to think she might not die today.

She shouldered the red bag that contained her tools and sprinted up the corridor.

CHAPTER 2

"Jared, you baby. There's nothing to be afraid of."

Tiffany tugged at Jared's arm. In the moonlight, her long blonde hair seemed to shimmer, and the playful smile he'd fallen in love with practically glowed. In a bikini top and denim shorts, she was more irresistible than ever.

"I'm not afraid," Jared said. "Just exhausted."

He had every right to be. The two of them had been dropped off by a friend's ski boat at Fort Jefferson National Park, a pre-Civil War fortress on an isolated island key in the Dry Tortugas. The fort took up most of the key, leaving a beach and a campground outside the walls. They'd spent the day snorkeling and sunbathing. With midnight approaching, Jared's personal battery was about depleted. He didn't want to run it down to zero before he and Tiffany crashed in their tent. He'd spent the day eyeing Tiffany's bikini body, and he didn't want to fall asleep and let that go to waste.

"Ugh, seriously," Tiffany said. "Since graduation you've lost your spirit of adventure. Senior summer, baby. Maximize it. Let's go out to the point and watch the moon over the water."

The entire key was little more than a glorified sandbar. The eastern point was as far away as they could get from the campground without swimming.

"But I'm so beat," Jared said.

"Now you can stay here with the Shannons…" Tiffany pointed at the enormous tent the family of five had erected at the other end of the campground. "…or you could join your girlfriend for some fun."

She slipped a baggie of joints out of her pocket, pinched the sealed end between her fingers, and waved it before Jared. She laughed, and then took off running toward the point.

"Damn." A hot, stoned girl on a secluded beach in the dark wasn't anything he was going to pass up. He took off after her.

It took about two minutes to run out of island. Tiffany skidded to a stop in the sugary sand at the water's edge. The moon lit the beach and wave tips in a soft glow. Jared caught up, wrapped his arms around her waist, and reached into her pocket for the weed. She slapped his hand.

"No head start." She looked out to sea. "Look, is that a manatee?"

Offshore, something barely broke the surface and then submerged.

Jared squinted at the water. "Looks more like a log, maybe."

Something splashed in the water, closer, just a dozen yards out.

"It is. It's a manatee!"

Jared couldn't see much in the gloom. "Tiff, it could be anything. Even a shark."

"No way. A shark would have a big fin. It's a manatee, out by itself in the dark. It's probably scared, maybe trapped in fishing line or something."

Tiffany waded into the water. Thoughts of sea urchins, jellyfish and a dozen other painful animals came immediately to Jared's mind.

"Tiff, get out of there. It's dangerous."

"You're going to let a helpless animal suffer? You have really gone lame."

Any hope of beach tent sex began to evaporate. He couldn't very well stay back now that Tiffany had plunged forward. He followed her in.

"Here, little boy," Tiffany called out to sea.

She waded in waist-deep, and then swam out a few yards. Jared stopped as water rose to his chest and sent a shiver up his spine.

A giant claw burst out of the water beside Tiffany. It had to be six feet long and nearly as wide. In the moonlight, it seemed almost transparent.

Tiffany screamed.

The claw snapped open and lunged. It clamped around her waist and jerked her under the water. The sea swallowed her bubbling cry for help, and then she went silent.

Terror ripped through Jared like a bolt of lightning. He panicked, turned, and ran. Or tried to. In the deeper water, every step felt like wading through molasses. His feet sank into the sand. He struggled to go faster but it felt as if the entire ocean wanted to hold him back, to make him a meal for whatever giant crustacean had just taken his girlfriend.

A thunderous splash sounded behind him. His foot crashed against coral and ripped the skin from his toes. He stumbled and went underwater.

A rock-hard claw clamped across his back and chest. He screamed and sucked in sea water. The claw wrenched him up and into the air. He coughed and shook the water from his eyes.

He hung face to face with a giant crab. It reeked like a rancid fish. Black eyes on short stalks stared into his. Its mandibles opened to expose a dark, hungry mouth.

The crab swallowed Jared whole.

CHAPTER 3

It was only ten in the morning on Garden Key and the place had been hot as an oven for over an hour. Fort Jefferson's eastern face was already warm to the touch.

Park Service Ranger Kathy West adjusted her campaign hat around her short brown ponytail, put on her sunglasses, and stepped out from the shade of the fort's main gate. It felt like she'd stepped into a solar flare. The island had scant natural shade, and with the reflected light off the sand and the sea coming in from all sides, it was easy to empathize with a piece of seared fish.

She looked over at the key's sole dock. The ferry from Key West would arrive soon. To the passengers, during the approach the fort would appear to rise directly from the water, three massive stories of deep red brick that stretched out for thousands of feet on every side. The ferry would deliver tourists for the day, and extract last night's campers with them in the afternoon. Visitors would get a tour of the fort, more time on the broiling beach than they could stand, lunch on the ferry, and a two-hour trip back home to their Key West hotels.

Ranger Reuben Harney stepped up behind Kathy. He only came up to her shoulder, but at her height, most people did. He wore civilian clothes.

"I feel like I'm shirking duty dressed like this," he said.

"According to Park Headquarters, you're officially reassigned to Denali National Park as of today. Have a nice ferry ride. Oh, and enjoy the snow up there."

Reuben faked a shiver. "Yeah, that might take some getting used to. But I think the staff might take more getting used to."

"That park is way bigger than our little island here. You'll finally have more than one other ranger to keep you company, and you won't have to live in technological isolation."

"That wasn't what I meant. I meant it was great working with you. I'd been trapped in administration before this assignment. You taught me a lot about living in the park, respecting the wildlife, respecting the history, and trying to pass that respect on to the visitors each day."

Kathy slapped him on the shoulder. "You getting all misty-eyed on me? You do that up at Denali, your eyes will freeze over."

Reuben looked sheepish. "Nah, just being appreciative. Things that ought to be said ought to be said."

"Well, you did great work here. I was happy to recommend you for the new posting. Go finish packing. You miss the ferry and you'll be stuck here another night, and your replacement will have already arrived and moved into your apartment. I need to go give a big welcome to Nathan Quincy Toland, historian."

"How long has he been a ranger?"

"I think he's still measuring it in days."

"You'll be a good one to break him in."

Kathy started to feel embarrassed at the praise. "Why don't you get back to packing before I make you give the fort tour."

Reuben smiled. "Yes, ma'am. Right away, ma'am."

Kathy headed for the dock. The daily ferry was the only way to traverse the seventy miles back to Key West. Two small dock houses and the pier serviced the ferry, and the remains of two coaling stations stood at the key's far north and south. Bush Key stretched out to the east for a few thousand yards with Long Key pointing south at the end of it. Shifting sand had long ago joined all three into one island, ironically shaped like a skeleton key.

Kathy thought that Fort Jefferson was a great place for Nathan to get started. No mega wildlife like Yellowstone, no huge crowds like Yosemite, no precipitous cliffs like Grand Canyon. Rangers carried a sidearm per policy, but using it hadn't crossed Kathy's mind since she'd arrived. This was the perfect location for her to ease Nathan into the ranger life.

She stepped onto the dock as the ferry arrived for its five-hour stay. The ship docked, and a crew member disembarked and handed her the manifest. Twenty-one visitors and no campers. That meant one less worry that evening. She and the new ranger would have the island to themselves as long as no private boaters arrived during the day. She didn't see Nathan's name on the list.

The passengers disembarked. Several looked a bit green from seasickness. Three had no hats. They'd regret that soon, especially the middle-aged bald man in the red Hawaiian shirt. Everyone looked like they were eager to get started. She looked for the replacement ranger, but everyone wore beach clothes. Perhaps he'd missed the ferry. That would be a bad way to start his first assignment.

"I'm Ranger West," she said to the crowd. "Welcome to Fort Jefferson. We'll do a detailed tour of the fort in a bit, but I'm just covering the basics first. There's no water on the island and no food for sale. There is no cell service and no power or landlines back to the mainland. If you have to go, there are composting toilets near the campground."

"Eww," a teenage girl said.

"Hey, you're just here for a few hours," Kathy said. "I live here."

The crowd laughed.

"This is an unforgiving environment," Kathy continued. "Watch the sun. You can already see it's brutal. Stay hydrated. Above all, don't miss the ferry for the trip back at three p.m. Because another thing we don't have here is a hotel."

The group laughed again. Kathy smiled, energized by getting people interested in her park. She headed for the fort and they followed.

"Fort Jefferson was built before the Civil War to protect trading vessels off the Florida coast on their way to New Orleans and Mobile. When steam replaced sail, it also served as a coaling station. The remnants of those stations are big open concrete pads north and south of the fort. The north pad is where we store a lot of the scrap left over from decades of Navy occupation, and it's off limits."

They approached the fort. Almost two hundred years old, it still elicited hushed 'wows' from the visitors.

"The fort is a pentagon, equal on all sides. We're going to walk across a moat and through the main and only gate. The thick oak doors are reproductions, but the hardware is original."

She led the group into the old parade ground in the fort's open center. A few trees dotted the grassy expanse. "You can explore any part of the fort you like. Spiral staircases lead from the first to the second tier, and up to the roof, or terreplein."

"Are those real cannons up there?" asked a little boy in a Donald Duck T-shirt.

"Yes, there are ten restored Rodman cannons on the terreplein. We fire blanks from them on special occasions."

The boy's eyes went wide.

"But don't get your hopes up," Kathy said. "Today isn't one of those occasions."

The little boy drooped.

"After checking out the fort, you're free to wander the rest of the key. The beaches have great snorkeling. Enjoy yourselves."

The group shuffled off. One man remained behind, a geeky twenty-something in baggy shorts and sandals. Bushy dark hair framed sparkling brown eyes. A backpack hung from one shoulder. He approached with an open hand and a big smile.

"Ranger West, I'm Nathan Toland."

Kathy shook his hand. "It's Kathy. Welcome to Fort Jefferson. You weren't on the manifest."

"Kind of threw the dude checking me in when I didn't have a return ticket. Said his arriving and departing counts had to match. So I told him to just leave me off, and that seemed to solve his problem."

"It's tough to get good help." She looked Nathan's tourist-style clothes up and down. "Trying to sneak in undercover?"

"I had my uniform on at first," he said. "Then I got spooked. I was afraid that people would start asking me about their upcoming day at the fort, and I'd seem pretty foolish not knowing any answers."

"Don't you have…?" She looked out the gate and saw a huge red suitcase on the dock. "…any luggage, I was going to say."

"Travelling light, but I have uniforms and everything on the recommended packing list."

"That's good, because as you can see, we can't run out to Walmart if we need anything. Do you have a sidearm in that bag?"

"No. I wasn't slated to attend the law enforcement academy. Never been that comfortable around modern firearms. But muzzle-loading cannons? Totally up my alley."

"We have a few of those. You'll be in charge of repelling pirates." She walked him back to the ranger quarters, two apartments built beside the western wall of the fort. "So, this is your first assignment. Were you driven here by a fascination to get off the grid?"

"No, more by my historian's fascination with the past."

"There are straight historic parks to work at, like Ford's Theater or Bull Run."

Nathan's eyes lit up. "Every park has history, every park is part of our history, one and the same. For me, Fort Jefferson's attraction is the richness of its undiscovered past. The place just faded away, like its life story had been silted over. My goal is to spend my off hours here writing the fort's definitive biography."

"Good news, there aren't many distractions. Bad news, there also aren't any research resources. You heard my 'no internet' warning to the visitors. That's true for us as well."

"No worries." He slapped his backpack. "I've downloaded thousands of documents, cataloged thousands more, all waiting to be tapped on my hard drive."

"Then as long as our generator keeps making electricity, you'll be fine. Go to the far apartment and unpack. Reuben is packing this morning, and he leaves on the ferry today. You have until three p.m. to absorb all his knowledge. Tomorrow, the history spiel I gave today will be all yours."

"Awesome! I was so excited, I had hardtack for breakfast."

"You had what?'

"Hardtack. A positively miserable cracker you have to break with a hammer and soak in water before you can eat it."

"And you ate in because...?"

"That's what Civil War soldiers ate. I like to immerse myself in the history of a place, do things the people of the time would have. This morning, I ate like a soldier in Fort Jefferson."

"And how was it?"

Nathan sprouted a big grin. "Absolutely awful. Which was perfect!"

"Don't expect me to join you in that ritual tomorrow morning."

"No worries. So, how is it you ended up at Fort Jefferson?"

"My background is in biology. The island is surrounded by a marine sanctuary including a nurse shark breeding area. I'd spent my first decade with the Park Service in mountains and forests, it was time to see the ocean."

"And how's it working for you?"

"Exactly what I was looking for after the stress of bigger parks. This is probably the most peaceful, quiet park in the system. Nothing out of the ordinary ever happens out here."

CHAPTER 4

When the ferry departed that afternoon, all the day trippers had checked back in. Many looked like roasted chickens, especially the bald man in the Hawaiian shirt, who had resorted to making a paper hat out of NPS brochures. The family of salt-encrusted campers also boarded, burdened with all their gear. They'd only stayed overnight, but the Shannons had packed in every modern convenience they could. Kind of missing the point of camping as far as Kathy was concerned.

Reuben hadn't missed his ride back to civilization, and he and Kathy had shared a heartfelt goodbye before the ferry pulled up the gangplank.

Only after the ferry had sailed away did Kathy realize something had slipped through the cracks. Distracted by Reuben's departure, she hadn't realized one set of campers scheduled to depart hadn't. Two teenagers who'd just graduated high school. They had been dropped off by personal boat but were scheduled to return by ferry. If any group would be irresponsible enough to miss the only ride home, that would be the one.

She headed over to the campsites. The official designation gave the location more credit than it deserved as it was just an open, sandy area, though a few rusting barbeques and a stand of bushes stuck out of the sand in defiance of nature. The circus tent that the Shannon family had erected was gone. She didn't see any other tents. She recalled that the kids had set up on the other side. She walked over to their location.

Their tan tent was still there, collapsed on the ground and partially covered by windswept sand. She picked one corner up and shook it clean. A great split rent the nylon down the middle. The tent was one of the cheapest models, practically disposable. She wondered if it had even lasted the night with two active teens inside of it.

She started a search out along Bush Key. The incoming tide sent waves lapping up over the sand. Further up above the high tide line, it looked like there were two sets of footprints, but the way they stepped on each other, it was hard to tell.

She reached the end of the key. The footprints stopped here. But that didn't mean anything. The teens, if these *were* their footprints, could have walked back along the beach that had been exposed at low tide. Or these could have been prints from the Shannon family, or day trippers.

If the missing had been a family, or a group of adults, Kathy might have had a different, more ominous, take on the situation. But being careless teens made different, less dire scenarios plausible. Maybe through some act of stupidity they'd ripped a hole in the tent, so they just left it here, rather than lug it home. Maybe the wind uncovered the ruined tent they'd buried, instead of partially covering one they'd never returned to. Perhaps their friends with the boat had picked them back up, and the ferry reservation had been a back-up plan.

Then again, maybe she'd been too distracted by Reuben's send off to notice that they'd gotten on the ferry after all.

There was a lot of circumstantial evidence that could point either way. She'd hate to risk having the Park Service look foolish by issuing an alert about two teens who were home safe in bed.

An old cabin cruiser rode at anchor off the point. The twenty-eight-footer had registered on arrival with Reuben and been there three days. A boat that small had a cabin the size of a dining room and little standing head room. A bit cramped for long-term living space for her taste.

If a boat had motored up and picked up those kids, whoever was on that cabin cruiser would have likely seen it.

Kathy decided to take the Park Service skiff out to the boat and see what light its captain might shine on this mystery.

CHAPTER 5

In the past, Fort Jefferson had hosted the finest ships in the United States Navy. Under the Park Service, the floating contingent had been reduced to one twelve-foot metal jon boat pushed by an aging nine-horsepower outboard. Strictly usable for circumnavigating the key, only the foolhardy would use it to traverse the seventy miles back to Key West.

Kathy nosed the skiff through a light chop and toward the cabin cruiser. The closer she got, the more the pleasure boat showed its age. Glaze and pitting marred the cabin windows and the bridge windscreen above. Paint peeled from the hull, and barnacles and seaweed clung to the boat's stained waterline. Sunlight had baked the once rich wooden deck to a parched gray. A winch worthy of a fishing trawler was mounted at the rear of the cockpit, and the extra weight made the boat list to starboard. The Park Service registration paperwork described the boat as a 1968 Owens 28, the owner as Marc Metcalf.

As she closed on the cruiser, Kathy throttled back the engine. Marc's head popped up from the cabin. The wizened little man had to be over eighty years old. The breeze ruffled his bush of frazzled gray hair. Several days of silver stubble covered cheeks tanned to leather from years of tropical sun. His purple T-shirt was on inside out, and Kathy thought possibly backward. He stood, closed the wooden door to the cabin, and slid a lock into a latch.

Marc closing up the cabin as she approached was not a good sign. Kathy cut the engine to idle as she came up on the stern. The skiff slowed to a stop. Faded letters spelled out the name *Solitude*. A rusting ladder hung beside the name. She straightened her campaign hat.

"Mr. Metcalf? I'm Ranger Kathy West. Maybe you can help me out?"

Marc sat down in the rear of the cockpit and leaned on the tiller. "Most likely." His voice had the reedy, crackling quality old age engendered.

Not being invited aboard was Bad Sign Number Two. She unsnapped her pistol's holster.

"You've been here three days, right?" she said.

"You betcha, and registered through three more. My fees are all paid up."

"I was wondering if you'd seen any boats come ashore near the campground or Bush Key last night or this morning."

"Nope, but I was dead asleep all night. Someone damage the reef?"

"Oh, no. Just might have picked up some campers."

Marc leaned over the transom. His blue eyes narrowed. "Someone's missing? Maybe more than one someone?"

Alarm bells rang in Kathy's head. That was a big leap for someone to make given the question she'd asked. "Did you see anything strange out here?"

"Lots of strange things happening out here." Marc pointed to the water. "And under there. Folks ain't ready to hear about none of it."

Kathy didn't like this guy's tin-foil-hat vibe. She rested her palm on the butt of her pistol. "Maybe I'm ready. Mind if I come on board to talk about it instead of shouting over my engine's noise?"

"That might be best," Marc said.

Kathy goosed the throttle and nudged the skiff alongside the cruiser. She killed the engine and tossed Marc the bow line. He tied it off to a cleat and she climbed onboard up the rear ladder. The cockpit was bare save for two square blue cushions. Stress cracks spider-webbed most of the paint.

"So what can you share with me?" Kathy said.

Marc's eyes flitted around the boat, then out across the sea, as if checking that they were still alone. "These are dangerous waters."

"You mean for ships or for people?"

"For everything."

"Around the fort is pretty safe. Sharks are rare, except the harmless nurse sharks. Man-of-war jellyfish season has passed. A little sharp coral scraping some feet is the worst I see."

"You ain't looking as hard as I am."

Marc rose, and with shaking hands, opened up the cabin hatches. He stepped down inside and motioned for Kathy to follow him. She peered inside.

The interior looked more like the bridge of a submarine. Electronics filled the cabin. Sonar screens, hydrophones, and a lot of other equipment she couldn't identify. A nautical chart of the Florida Keys covered the forward bulkhead. Pins with various colored flags dotted the map. Marc took a seat on an upside-down plastic milk crate in front of a sonar display.

"That's a hell of a fish finder you have there, Mr. Metcalf."

"Call me Marc, and this ain't no fish finder. It's mostly last-generation Navy cast-offs, but that don't mean it ain't good."

"If you aren't looking for fish, what are you looking for?"

"Crabs. Giant crabs."

"The Keys don't have any large crab species."

"I didn't say large. I said *giant*. Bigger than this boat giant."

Kathy realized she may have just gotten on the ship to Crazy Island. "Really?"

"Been stories of them passed down for hundreds of years. I'm searching for them, or for where they live, making the most detailed maps there are of the waters around the Keys. I gotta convince people to stop 'em before they kill again. But from what you're saying, they may have already started."

"I didn't say anyone had been killed. And there's a big gulf between a giant crab legend and reality."

"I've done crossed that gulf, Ranger. I know what I know. The question is, are you ready to know it?"

CHAPTER 6

Kathy sat on the top step between the cockpit and the cabin. She judged Marc as more sun-fried brain than delusional-dangerous. No harm in letting him continue his tale. "Tell me what you know."

"If you can stand a personal question, when was you born?"

"1990."

"Let me tell you a story that's before your time," Marc said. "Hell, it's before your parents' time.

"It was the spring of 1961. I was an Arkansas kid, just eighteen, no college draft deferment in my pocket. So I joined the Coast Guard, thought at least I'd get stationed on a beach somewheres. I was an idiot.

"Now south of here, Fidel Castro was working overtime to turn Cuba into a new protectorate of the Soviet Union, and that didn't sit well with no one. So the CIA hatches a plan they call Operation Zapata, what folks now call the Bay of Pigs Invasion."

"I've read a little about that. Cuban exiles tried to overthrow Castro?"

"About 1,500 of them, with some light tanks, supported by World War II-era bombers and a hodgepodge of naval vessels. All run by the CIA with the President's approval and the President's promise of total denial if the whole show went up in flames."

"Which it did."

"Gloriously," Marc said.

"Kind of seems stupid from the start, trying to take over a country with 1,500 soldiers."

"Yes indeedy. And that's because the human invasion was only half the CIA's plan. The other half was a non-human invasion by giant crabs."

Kathy stared at him. "You know that sounds like a bad science fiction story."

"Mine ain't fiction. It's factual. I fought 'em."

"What?"

"As part of the run-up to the Bay of Pigs, my Coast Guard unit gets re-assigned. The brass outfits us with old Navy PT boats from World War II. Big wooden launches with twin .50 machine guns in two turrets and upgraded to two new torpedoes along each side. Mine was PT 904. The boats might be old, but they are fitted with the latest fish. Mark 45 torpedoes, brand new and wire-guided. We have 'em before any ships in the Navy did. They train us to maintain everything but the warheads. Only later I found out these fish were nuclear-capable, designed to sink Russian submarines."

"You were on a boat carrying six nuclear warheads?"

"We never heard nothing about being nuclear. We assumed they had conventional warheads. But things were pretty wild back then, sky's the limit thinking. World War II boats carrying low-yield Cold War nukes? Crazy enough to have happened.

"Anyway, we trained in the Louisiana bayous, then in March we sail out to the Keys. Now no one tells us the mission, but I mean, Cuba's only a hundred damn miles away, so it ain't hard to figure out. Eventually command spills the beans. Our job was going to be to sink any Cuban vessels that respond to the invasion. The regular Navy was a bit too large of a presence to allow what they called 'plausible deniability,' and our little boats can sneak in and out.

"So it's the last week in March and my boat and PT 906 are riding at anchor one night off Loggerhead Key. Now we're still kinda the Coast Guard so we have ammo for the twin .50s up front. We're carrying four Mark 45 torpedoes but we haven't had no practice with 'em yet. Orders are to rise at dawn the next day for training southeast of Key West. So Tommy Greaves, Bud Sterling, Matty Kite, and me are racked out on 904, same as the fellas on the other boat.

"It's 0200 or so and the sea is pancake flat. I'm sleeping like a newborn when this crash and screams from the other boat wake me up so fast I slam my skull into the bulkhead. We all end up on deck and I hit the bow spotlight."

"The other PT is stern high, damn near vertical, new props all shiny in the light. Then it sinks. Now I've seen plenty of ships sink. There's a slow-motion aspect, a grace to it. This PT ain't got no grace. The thing sinks beneath the waves like it's being pulled under. Snap, yank, gone. Then there's nothing. Not a sound, not a bubble. No survivors.

"We're cursing and confused because we got no clue what just happened. So Tommy and Bud head for the .50s. Matty goes to the bow to raise anchor. I twist the switch and fire up the engines. The PT roars to life, and I mean roar. Sweet Jesus that boat was loud.

"Matty's pulling up the anchor line like he's inspired by the Devil and Tommy and Bud are slapping the .50s into action when there's this surge in the water off the bow. I've still got the area lit like center ring at the circus. Then something breaks surface on both sides of the bow. I can't tell what it is, can't see nothing really, like whatever it is it's invisible. But the waves rock the boat and the spotlight arcs across the thing. The reflection off the wet surface is the outline of two giant crab claws. Six feet long, easy.

"I shout for Matty to cut the anchor line and I slam the boat into reverse. Tommy and Bud open fire at point-blank range, each aiming at the claw on their side of the boat.

"Now a .50 is a big round. I mean, it'll tear an arm clean off, punch a hole through a hull. But these bullets just bounce off those damn claws.

"Now here the props dig in, the bow rises, and the boat starts backward. Then in full illumination, spotlight dead center, I see the most awful thing. One claw opens, sweeps in, and cuts Matty in two at the waist. His upper half drops into the sea. His legs stand for what seem like forever until they fall over.

"Tommy and Bud both scream, but out of fury, not some girly scream, you know. They keep pouring on the .50s until the barrels glow and the magazines go empty. The claws drop back into the sea.

"The boat picks up speed and I swing the bow around to starboard because I have no intention on backing up all the way to Key West. Problem is, Matty pulled in the anchor line, but never uncleated it. I'm doing ten knots-plus when the line playing out over the bow goes taut. The anchor wedges into some coral or something and the force rips the cleat right off the bow, along with a nice chunk of the deck. That yanks us back to a dead stop.

"Tommy and Bud are scrambling to find the spare magazines, because we weren't even contemplating combat, let alone giant crabs. Then the claws come back up, one on either side amidships. They reach in and yank both fellas right out of the turrets like dolls, and throw them into the sea.

"I'll admit that right then I'm not thinking. It's all panic mode with three buddies dead, a PT boat sunk, and a giant crab on the attack. I throw the boat into full speed ahead, hoping maybe I could run the damn thing over."

"The boat never gets the chance. Both claws blast out of the water portside. One grabs the bow, the other amidships. Then a giant crab pulls itself out of the sea. 904 was seventy-two feet long and this thing took up half her side. It crawls up onto the deck, nearly transparent, but undeniably there in the spotlight's glare. The thing stinks like a rotting carcass.

"The boat can't take the extra weight. With every foot the crab climbs up, 904 lists further and further to port. The sound of cracking wood rips through the air. When water washes over the gunwale, I know I'm screwed and we're going turtle. I climb out of the wheelhouse and grab a life jacket on the way to the starboard side. By now, the side of the ship's practically straight up. I stand on the edge of the boat and jump. Just as I do, old 904 snaps in half. I hit the water and swim away.

"Behind me, the crab pulls the PT under. The engines gurgle and stop. Water leaks into the spotlight as it sinks and it explodes underwater with this muted pop.

"Then there's nothing. No sound, no light, no motion. Just me treading water in the Caribbean, the night so dark I can't tell where the sea stops and the sky begins."

Marc paused and then shook his head. "Everything happened so damn fast. I'd only been awake for five minutes, and I seen seven men killed and two boats sunk by a giant crab."

Kathy gripped the hem of her pants in anticipation. "How long were you in the water?"

"Not long. I swam to Loggerhead Key before sunrise. We had this murky chain of command and I wasn't sure how many people knew where we was, or would miss us if we didn't get to training the next day. But a little after noon, an all-black helo flies in, circles the key, and picks me up. Everyone inside's wearing suits, full-fledged spooks. I tell them what happened on the way back to Key West."

"Did they believe you?" Kathy asked.

"Yeah, like they was expecting it, not a bit of surprise."

"Did they pass it up the chain of command?"

"All the way to the top. Literally. From Key West, they drive me to some secure place in the Everglades. I sit in something way too similar to solitary confinement for hours, then get ushered into a conference room. There's a bunch of suits, and Army and Air Force generals, and Navy and Coast Guard admirals. A map of Cuba and the surrounding waters hangs on the wall, with labeled yellow flags pinned all over it. I notice the two flags at Loggerhead Key were black. The kicker? At the head of the table sits the President."

"Of the United States?"

"John Fitz Kennedy himself. The Coast Guard admiral orders me to report on the mission. Kennedy cuts him off."

"'So, sailor, you've been patrolling in a PT boat?' he asks me. He had that same smile that won him an election."

"I say 'yes' and we talk PT boats for a minute or so. He gets kind of wistful, because you know that's what he commanded in World War II. Then he asks about the crab and I tell him, tell him how one boat sank before I knew it, how I watched my three buddies die before the thing crushed my boat. When I talk about the ship sinking out from under me, tears well in his eyes, I think because his ship was crushed under a Japanese destroyer in the war.

"When I finish, he's quiet. The whole room, filled with all these powerful people, I can feel their anticipation as he steeples his fingers together and stares at the map.

"'We can't unleash those,' he says. 'They are not controllable.'

"One of the guys in a suit offers that that was the point. A natural disaster, something to get the Cuban military to react to before the invasion, and a pretext for Operation Zapata, exiles coming home to keep the crabs from spreading over the island.

"Kennedy won't hear it. He says this was Eisenhower's plan, not his, and he was barely comfortable with the military side, let alone the cockamamie 'science fiction' half of the plan.

"At that point, the two admirals realize I was still there, and have me ushered out. I'm threatened with a minimum of life in prison and a maximum of death for treason if I ever breathe a word of this story to anyone. Now I hope the statute of limitations has run out on that threat."

"That's a hell of a story," Kathy said.

"Ain't no story. The truth. After I got out of the service, I moved back here. Spent my life hopping around marinas, doing boat repairs, scraping barnacles, charter fishing, whatever came up. The off days I'm out here."

Kathy sighed. "Looking for giant crabs."

"You betcha."

"Find any?"

"Since you ain't never heard about them until now, the answer's no, ain't it?" He shook his head. "Ah, I can see it in your eyes. Crazy old man in his leaky old boat."

"Not at all."

"The last week, there's been motion on the sea floor. I seen it on the sonar. Too big and dense to be schools of fish. Just the right size to be them crabs. You got missing kids. I've got your suspect. You don't want to put 'em together, then that's on you."

At this point, all Kathy wanted was to escape this floating madhouse of conspiracy theories. The old man had her listening, but incredulous, up through the crab attack. But meeting Kennedy had been one layer of icing too thick.

"I need to head back and keep the tourists in line," Kathy said. "My partner will think I'm lost at sea. Thank you for all you've told me, and if you find anything out here, let me know."

She reached over to shake his hand. He gave it a weak attempt.

"Didn't expect you'd believe me," he said, looking at the deck. "But at my age, I figured someone had to know. Can't live forever."

Kathy didn't know what to say to that. She backed out of the gloomy cabin and into the cockpit's pounding daylight. A minute later, she was pointing the skiff back to Fort Jefferson, and away from the poor man with the giant crab delusions.

CHAPTER 7

By six p.m., purple-black clouds had blotted out the sky's Caribbean blue. The evening vowed to be loud, windy, and wet.

Pop-up tropical showers were the island's norm, but tonight a cold front had swept down from the north, and the collision of northern cool air with southern steamy moisture promised a sustained set of storms. The good news was that the day's tourists had already departed on the ferry, and they'd be back at Key West by now.

Kathy walked across the courtyard of the fort and gave the sky a trepidatious look. Radioing in to Park Headquarters about the vague possibility of missing teens that afternoon hadn't sat well with her. An incoming storm made her mood as dark as the sky threatened to become.

Of all the places to be in a big storm, Fort Jefferson was one of the safest. Secure behind feet of brick walls, Kathy could stay dry through a hurricane. If she sat in the thick-walled powder magazine on the parade ground's north end, she probably couldn't even hear the thunder.

Nathan met her under an arch on the other side of the fort. Worry creased his face. "Weather Service posted a severe thunderstorm warning for us."

"The sky concurs."

"Anything special we do?"

"The day trippers are gone and we have no campers," Kathy said. "The skiff is up on the beach. We just hunker down and ride it out. Before we get soaked, the light show from the terreplein is usually pretty good."

"Without television or the internet, that qualifies as some major entertainment."

Kathy led Nathan up to the roof of the fort. No longer blocked by the walls, the stiff wind carried in the damp smell of impending rain, and rippled their pants against their legs.

Nathan stepped over to one of the restored Rodman cannons. Cannonballs stood stacked beside it. The rear of the cannon's carriage had wheels that rested on an arc of painted iron. He gave it a shove. The cannon pivoted an inch to the left.

"Whoa! These really are restored with a full traverse along the field of fire."

"Yes, the restoration team went overboard. You'll get to fire one on the Fourth of July."

Nathan raised a fist in triumph. "Excellent! A fair trade for a year without internet access."

Out to the west, the clouds darkened to black. Flashes of lightning backlit them, followed by the low roll of thunder. A mile or two away, a gray curtain of heavy rain stretched from the clouds to the sea.

"This is so awesome," Nathan said. "Can't you feel the history?"

"No, just a few raindrops."

"Seriously? Don't you think of all the people since before the Civil War who stood right here, who waited for the rain, especially when it was the only source of water? We're part of this whole time-continuum."

"I guess so. I'm so preoccupied with the safety of our visitors and the wildlife we protect that I forget this place has so much history. I really haven't researched the fort's past other than what's in the visitor's guide," Kathy said. "Reuben covered all that. My background is biology, not history."

"Oh, then you're totally missing out," Nathan said. "The history is fascinating."

Kathy had rarely ever put the words "history" and "fascinating" together, and never with Nathan's level of exuberance.

Nathan pointed to the south. "After the War of 1812, the country realizes it's vulnerable to a seaborne invasion by a greater power, which is just about anyone at that point. The government starts building this string of forts to guard harbors, real brick monsters. Southern ones like Fort Sumter and Fort Morgan will become famous decades later in the Civil War when the U.S. Navy has to re-take its property from the Confederacy."

He swept his hands wide apart. "This fort was a masterpiece. Four hundred and fifty guns, pointing in all directions, ready to blast any ship stupid enough to approach."

"Anyone ever test that theory?"

"No way. No foreign power ever dared approach Fort Jefferson, and the fort was too far out at sea for Confederate forces to care about, even if they'd had a real navy. In fact, during the war, this place became a prison, housing criminals and Confederate POWs."

Kathy looked out at the desolate key. "A deterrent to capture, certainly."

"Being here will really bring depth to my history of the fort."

Kathy didn't think that sounded like a best seller outside a few historians.

"Who do you think the most famous prisoner was?" Nathan asked.

"I do know that one. Samuel Mudd, the doctor that set John Wilkes Booth's broken leg after the Lincoln assassination."

Nathan looked a bit crestfallen at not being the one to make the revelation. Then his face brightened. "But you know what I found? Letters he wrote from this prison. Never delivered to his family."

"Because…?"

"The commander was afraid the letters would get him released."

"How?"

"Mudd writes several times about seeing giant crabs on the beach at night."

Kathy rolled her eyes. "Great, another giant crab story. You need to swim out to Marc on his cabin cruiser and swap tall tales."

She went on to relay Marc's wild conspiracy story about the CIA and giant crabs gone wild.

"I so want to interview that dude," Nathan said. "He's living history."

"Maybe living in his own version of the world, as well."

"Well, yeah, the story's bizarre," Nathan said. "But the giant crab myth is common throughout the Keys. Now, Mudd didn't know that, and claimed to see crabs fifteen feet wide."

"Marc's story says thirty feet wide. Inflation, I guess."

"Mudd saw them crawl up out of the water at full moon high tides and strip the area of any vegetation or wildlife they could catch. He said the soldiers were sworn to secrecy about it."

"Didn't other prisoners see them?"

"Mudd worked as an unpaid doctor, so he got a little more freedom of movement. None of the others were out in the fort at night. The fort commander held the letters, fearing if they got out, Mudd's family would use them to try and prove he was insane and get him released on those grounds."

"Ever considered that maybe he was nuts, and the isolation out here didn't make him any better?"

"I hoped being here would help me put his letters in context. I think—" Nathan paused and pointed to the northwest. "Hey, what's that out there?"

Over half a mile out to sea, the wind had beaten the water into white-capped-swells. A long yellow sea kayak appeared and disappeared between the waves. In the rear seat, a woman flailed with a two-headed paddle. The gray curtain of rain followed close behind her.

In the race to the shore between her and the thunderstorm, she was going to lose.

CHAPTER 8

"Damn it," Kathy said.

She ran down to her quarters on the ground floor and returned with a set of binoculars. She trained them west and scanned the sea. She saw nothing but frothing water.

"Where the hell did that kayak go?" she said.

"There," Nathan said. "Farther left."

She angled left and saw bright yellow. She adjusted the focus and a sea-going kayak sharpened into clarity. A red bundle filled the front seat. In the back seat, a woman in a green tank top flailed against the sea with a long two-headed paddle. She didn't have a hat or a lifejacket. Even at this distance, Kathy could see the exertion had colored her face beet-red.

"A kayak." She handed the binoculars to Nathan.

"Whoa. What is she doing out this far?" Nathan handed her back the binoculars.

Kathy checked the kayaker again. "Idiots do idiotic things. She doesn't even have a life jacket on." She shoved the binoculars against Nathan's chest. "Raise the Coast Guard. The frequency is next to the radio."

"Where are you going?"

"To do something stupid, to save a stupid person, who is doing something even stupider."

Kathy ran down to the ground level, grabbed a green rain slicker from her quarters, and put it on as she sprinted to the skiff by the dock.

She glanced up in the direction she'd last seen the yellow kayak. Nothing but green water. She looked over her shoulder and up at Nathan on the terreplein. He dropped the binoculars from his eyes and pointed west-southwest. He looked grim.

Kathy pushed the boat off the beach, stern-first. The wind-driven waves slapped against the transom and pushed the boat back to shore. It was as if the sea itself was delivering a final warning that should she venture from land, there was no guarantee she'd return.

She gave the boat a stronger shove out to sea, and then pulled herself aboard. She crawled back to the outboard and yanked the starter cord. The engine roared to life and she snapped it into reverse.

The little boat struggled. Water slammed the transom and splashed Kathy's face. She spun the boat around and headed out into the waves.

Two lifejackets peeked out from under the seat and reminded her she was about to repeat one of the kayaker's mistakes. She put one on and moved the second so she'd have it ready for the rescue.

Salt spray stung her eyes. She wiped them and turned back to see Nathan. He pointed straight west, over her head. The boat slammed into a wave so hard it shuddered. She turned her face back into the wind and winced.

A half-dozen wave crests ahead, the kayak rose from the sea, nose pointing skyward. Then it scooted sideways down the swell and disappeared.

Huge, heavy drops of rain hit her boat like a handful of rocks. Sheet lightning unfurled across the sky. Then thunder cracked so sharp and so loud that Kathy involuntarily ducked.

The wall of rain raced across the surging sea, over where she'd seen the kayak, then the next instant, over her small boat. She turned to check for direction from Nathan, but the obscuring rain morphed the fort into a dark hulk.

Rainwater pooled around her feet. The boat labored up a wave and over the crest. As it headed down, the outboard's shaft rose from the water. The engine screamed. The boat plunged down and the prop again found purchase.

Kathy took the next wave at a slight angle. As she rode to the top, she saw nothing but rain against the wave tops. Down that wave, up the next, and still no kayak. Her heart pounded and she began to fear she had been too late.

Lightning flashed and struck the sea to her left. Another snap of thunder made her head ring. Water in her boat sloshed over her ankles.

From overhead came the whine of rotor blades. A red and white Coast Guard helicopter flew past her. It banked right and looped back around. A crewman crouched in the door wearing a wetsuit and a flight helmet. He pointed at Kathy, then made a circular motion with his hand and ended up pointing back to the fort. He made the same motion again, this time angrier.

Kathy knew he was right. They were the pros at this, not her. She had little more business out here than the kayaker did. And in another few minutes, she'd be just as bad off. She turned the skiff around and rode the waves back toward the fort. The wind and rain lashed her back, as if compelling her to keep going in that direction.

Behind her, the helicopter began a spiral search of the sea, an ever-widening circle to find the kayaker. The aircraft rocked in the gusty winds. The crewman hung out the open door, grasping a winch cable, searching the sea below.

Soon Kathy approached the dock. She couldn't risk slamming into the pilings. She cut the engine and the skiff surfed up onto the shore. She jumped out, relieved to be out of the pounding sea.

To the west, the helicopter circled the area where she'd last seen the kayak. She pulled the skiff ashore and shielded her eyes from the stinging rain. The helicopter made one more lap around the area, then peeled away, heading east. It flew over Kathy's head. The crewman looked down at her and shook his head as he passed.

Her heart sank. Maybe if she'd seen the kayaker earlier, started for her sooner… But those kayaks were supposed to be unsinkable. To have one disappear beneath the waves...

She cursed and kicked a whelk shell back into the foaming sea. She was mad at herself for failing, madder still at the idiot who put herself in that situation. Her feet slipped against the slick rocks as she trudged back to the fort, and shelter from the storm. Nathan met her at the entrance as she stepped out of the rain.

"I…I couldn't find her," Kathy said.

"Not your fault," Nathan said. "She disappeared, the whole kayak disappeared before you got halfway out."

"If I'd seen her earlier…"

"You might not have realized it being in that little boat, but you were lucky to get back alive. You surfed in ahead of some swells that would have swamped the skiff."

Now she realized why the Coast Guardsman was so mad. She had been about to make his job twice as hard.

"I need to go get dry," she said, "and get some hot coffee."

"I'll put on a pot in the office. First round is on me."

CHAPTER 9

That night Nathan marveled at the events of his first day at Fort Jefferson.

He felt awful about the kayaker lost at sea. Park rangers weren't search-and-rescue professionals, and that woman had no business being out in that weather, but he still wished there had been a better outcome. In training, the instructors had told a lot of stories about NPS rescues in some of the more dangerous locations like Grand Canyon and Denali. With only a handful of day visitors at Fort Jefferson, he'd thought life-threatening emergencies would be the least of his problems. Now he knew better.

While he loved the history of the place, he had to admit that he'd been worried about boredom or island claustrophobia setting in over time. If every day was going to be this active, neither of those would be a problem.

Tomorrow, he'd lead his first historical tour of the fort. He'd long memorized the key points around the fort and the short spiel he had time for at each one. Digging into the documents on his hard drive would prime him for his initial scrum of visitors.

When it came to his research, isolation would be one upside of being at Fort Jefferson. The daily distractions of media and managing life chores would not be interfering with the work. The isolation would also be the downside. The instant gratification of an internet search or wandering through a dusty archive were not going to happen. The best he was going to be able to do was plumb the depths of what he'd downloaded, then return to the mainland for another batch.

To get off to a good start, he'd downloaded quite a bit, enough to fill an auxiliary hard drive. He plugged it in and fired up his laptop.

"The best place to start," he said to himself, "is always at the beginning."

The beginning would be the early 1800s. Given the key's remoteness and the lack of fresh water, there had been no indigenous peoples on the island before Spain ceded Florida to the fledgling United

States. The basic history said that Commodore David Porter was the first naval officer to survey the keys known as the Dry Tortugas. Nathan began his search with David Porter.

His only hit was the commodore's ship logbook. The original 1825 book had been scanned and entered into the database in its handwritten form, a shortcut for the person creating the database by not typing a transcription. Despite some legibility issues, Nathan loved it. Reading Porter's words in his own hand almost two hundred years later made Nathan feel closer to being there. He skimmed through pages of Porter's exploration of the Florida coast.

Porter sailed down the Florida Keys and gave Key West a lukewarm review, deeming the harbor potentially useful, but he was very wary about the coral shoals and cited the need to resupply it by ship from the mainland. Given the tropical heat and small size, he deemed it "impractical for habitation." Nathan thought the commodore would be quite amazed at how much "habitation" the island currently hosted.

The next pages contained the entry about the visit to what Porter called the chain's "further keys." Garden, Bush, Loggerhead. He was not impressed. Barren, too far from shipping lanes to be useful, too far away to even maintain a lighthouse. Nathan imagined Porter offering them back to Spain with a "thanks, but no thanks" note attached. He understood Porter's assessment. Without the fort, the treeless Garden Key was little more than a sand bar.

Chronologically, the next visit was four years later by Commodore Josiah Tattnall. His logbook was also in the database in its original form. Yellowed pages filled with a flowery script that put Porter's scrawl to shame. Tattnall's ship was out this far in the Gulf searching for an overdue vessel, the *U.S.S. Hamilton*. At the bottom of a page, he described finding the ship and noted the latitude and longitude coordinates. Nathan double-checked the location on a nautical map and it was on the shoals northwest of the fort.

The top of the next page began mid-sentence, and in a much tighter, hurried handwriting. Nathan flipped back to see if he'd missed something, but the PDF pages were in sequence. Along the logbook picture's left side, he could make out the jagged edge where a page had been torn out.

That was a big deal. Pages missing from the commodore's logbook, the most official document aboard ship, would have been a serious offense. For the book to survive this way, without any annotation, meant that it was entered as the official record knowing that it was incomplete. This was the nineteenth century equivalent of a redacted memo.

Tattnall's entry described the death of two survivors of the *Hamilton* from "irreversible exposure and dehydration" on board his ship. Then there followed a very detailed description of Bush Key and references to maps made by the crew.

The next day's entry is back in the earlier, open handwriting style. The entries are mundane, though the ship has reset course to bustling New Orleans, a destination further away than the ship's more isolated St. Augustine base. There is no further mention of the Keys.

Nathan leaned back in his chair. Historians loved to comb through the records in search of an oddity, and this certainly was one. Missing logbook pages and a radical change in course. Something happened out here. Something bad.

A page later, the ship docked in New Orleans and resupplied. Tattnall would have made a beeline for naval headquarters, but any records of what transpired there would be long gone.

The next mention of the Keys was in Tattnall's official report to Congress. He portrayed Garden and Bush Keys as critical to national defense, an outpost from which to launch patrols to safeguard American shipping in the area. The location Commodore Porter had earlier thought useless was now of the utmost importance.

Something on those missing pages had changed Tattnall's mind.

Nathan flipped back to the commodore's logbook. He read the list of supplies brought onboard in New Orleans. Gunpowder. Cannon balls. Fuses. A lot of them. Tattnall's ship had depleted its magazine while sailing in peacetime? The cash-strapped U.S. government wasn't in the habit of firing off ammo doing target practice.

A novel, exciting idea popped into Nathan's head. Perhaps the *U.S.S. Hamilton* had encountered pirates and ended up on the losing end of combat. Certainly Tatnall would not want to make public the weakness of the Navy to police its waters and would quickly move to have Congress bolster the area's defenses.

His heart skipped a beat at opening up a new chapter in America's history. A pirate attack, a government cover-up. He'd need a lot more corroborating evidence, most of it on the mainland, but such a revelation could shed a new light on a part of the nation's past that often lay forgotten, the years between the War of 1812 and the Civil War. Such a discovery would make waves in the community of historians.

Fort Jefferson National Park had always been considered a backwater. Pirates would certainly put it on the map. He couldn't think of anything happening out here more exciting than pirates.

CHAPTER 10

"How are you doing this morning?" Nathan asked.

He and Kathy were both working around the fort interior, sweeping and straightening, preparing the grounds for the arrival of the ferry full of tourists. Even low in the sky, the sun seemed to have already set the red bricks afire.

Kathy didn't want to weigh Nathan down with the burden of a full and truthful answer about a sleepless night and how poorly she was handling the kayaker's death. "Not bad."

"How about I greet the ferry today? Then walk everyone over to the fort and launch right into the history."

"No, I've got it."

"Seriously, just today. Decompress and I'll send them to you for the nature talk when I'm done."

The idea was appealing. She wasn't sure she could summon her best "Welcome-to-Fort-Jefferson" smile right now. She stopped sweeping.

"I'll take you up on that," she said. She leaned the broom against a wall. "I'll go walk the shoreline."

"I'll see you in a while then."

Kathy left the fort and hiked the shoreline, wanting to look down, but reflexively looking up, and out to sea. The sun had fired up the sky's turquoise shades in place of the deep early morning blue. The waters were empty. Marc Metcalf must have taken his battered little boat elsewhere in his giant crab search. Just as well that he missed the previous day's storm.

Near a curve in the shoreline, something large lay half-buried in the sand, one pointed end protruding. As the sun rose, its color brightened to a familiar, gut-wrenching yellow. The same color as yesterday's kayak.

Kathy approached the object. She grabbed the bow and rolled it up out of the sand. It was only the forward third of the boat. Deep gouges raked the sides where the waves had beaten it against the coral reef. The wider end looked as if it had been chopped off clean, like with a meat cleaver. The thick, hard plastic shell's edge was straight, almost polished. This kayak hadn't floundered, hadn't snapped in half. It appeared to have been cut.

She rooted around in the bow. Scraps of heavy fishing net stuck to the inner hull. This kayak had been part of a commercial fishing operation. Why would a woman in street clothes be seventy miles from civilization in a kayak from a fishing trawler? And why hadn't the trawler been here looking for her?

Kathy pulled the partial kayak further up on the beach. She searched the water and shoreline for the other half, or whatever pieces might have washed ashore. Further down the beach, she spied a sand-encrusted red nylon pack. It looked like the one the woman had tucked into the kayak's front seat.

She pulled the pack from the sand. Inside were wire cutters, screwdrivers, electrical tape, and an odd assortment of electronics. Who paddled out to sea carrying something like that?

A strange woman too far from land. A sabotaged or sliced kayak filled with all the wrong tools to take into the Gulf of Mexico. A heavy feeling in the pit of her stomach said that something very bad had already started unfolding.

CHAPTER 11

Nathan stood on the dock, faced the sun, and smiled. He'd given Kathy a little break and was about to greet his first group of visitors. The cloudless sky glowed a stunning blue and bright fish flickered in the water around the dock's pilings. He adjusted his campaign hat. This was going to be a good day.

His face shifted to a frown. He gave the waistline of his pants a twist. Today's dip into historical accuracy was a pair of period-accurate underwear. Knee-length woolen drawers with three buttons up the front. There was a good chance underwear made of fire ants would be more comfortable.

The ferry appeared and soon pulled up to the dock. It idled alongside the piling bumpers, then with a blast of reversed engines, went still. Compared to yesterday, it seemed oddly empty. Stranger still, no one disembarked to secure the ship.

One short man jumped from the ferry to the dock. He looked about fifty, with close-cut silver hair and the kind of face that looked hardened by the elements. His wrinkled blue suit stretched to cover a chest and arms that had spent a lot of hours in the gym. A battered sand-colored backpack hung from one shoulder. He locked steel-blue eyes on Nathan. Nathan suddenly felt like a guilty man before a hanging judge.

The ferry growled into reverse and churned the water white as it backed away. The sole passenger strode over to Nathan. Nathan didn't even think about launching into the welcome speech.

The man flipped open a leather case housing a badge and ID. "I'm Glen Larsson, Department of Homeland Security. You're Toland?"

"Uh, yeah. What are—?"

Larsson snapped closed his case and walked past Nathan toward the fort. "Where's West?"

"Walking the island." Nathan jogged a few steps to catch up with Larsson.

"No campers?"

"No. Whoa, what are you doing here?"

"DHS is temporarily closing the park." He loosened his tie as he walked. "Damn it's hot out here."

"Shouldn't the Park Service do that?"

"Son, on the real world power ladder, DHS is on the top rung."

They crossed the moat to the fort entrance.

"I must have missed something," Nathan said. "You think you can close us because of…?"

"NOAA alerted DHS of an incoming red tide. Does that sound like you should be open?"

Nathan could barely place that NOAA was the National Oceanic and Atmospheric Administration. He thought they tracked hurricanes. "Red tide?"

Larsson rolled his eyes. "A toxic algae bloom. Kills fish, sickens people. How can you not know what that is? You work at an oceanfront national park."

Nathan blushed. "I'm really more of a historian."

"Great. Well, to keep you from becoming part of some very bad future history of this place, the park is closed."

Nathan felt like he'd just been thrown in deep water. "Sorry. I've only been here a day."

"Well, son, you might have just picked the wrong day to take a job at the beach."

Larsson entered the fort and went straight for the restored powder magazine, a brick outbuilding on the parade ground's north side. He dropped the protective rope from the doorway and stepped in. "I'll use this room as a workspace."

"Whoa," Nathan said. "This room's filled with restored artifacts. We put the barriers up for a reason."

"I'll try not to break anything." Larsson's voice dripped with condescension. "I'll need about an hour to get organized and then I'll meet you and West in the main office."

As the man only carried a backpack, Nathan wondered what he'd need to get organized. Before he could ask, Larsson slammed the door in his face. From the other side, metal scraped on metal as an old deadbolt locked the door shut.

"First day on the job and I let a stranger close the park," Nathan whispered to himself. "This will not look good on my annual eval."

CHAPTER 12

Kathy looked across the key to see the newly arrived ferry headed back to sea. She got a sinking feeling in her gut. The boat was supposed to stay all day and bring the visitors back in the afternoon. It couldn't leave them all here.

She headed back to the fort at a jog. The main gate came into view and her sinking feeling dropped down below her knees. There should have been dozens of people milling around the entrance. She saw no one.

She entered the main gate and Nathan stood there, looking perplexed. The fort was empty.

"Where are all the visitors?" she asked.

"We've been closed. A dude from Homeland Security was the only one on the ferry. It dropped him and headed back to Key West."

"And why is Homeland Security here?"

"NOAA sent him to close the park ahead of the red tide."

"What the hell are you talking about? There's no red tide. It isn't even the right season for it. And why would NOAA contact DHS instead of the Park Service?"

"You know, the dude didn't seem open to any questions."

"Where is this man?"

"Went in the powder magazine and locked the door."

Kathy balled her fists so tight they went white. She marched straight to the magazine office. She pushed the door but it jammed against the deadbolt inside. The safety-versus-historical-accuracy debate about leaving it on the restored door had just been resolved in her mind. She banged on the door.

"Hey!" She realized she hadn't asked the man's name. "Homeland Security! This is Ranger West."

There was no answer. She slammed on the door a few more times. Something banged within the room. The deadbolt slid back and the door opened.

A short man in olive drab cargo pants and a tight black T-shirt opened the door. Sweat stippled his forehead under short, gray hair.

"Ranger West? I'm Derek Larsson, DHS."

"What are you doing in my park? Why did you send the ferry back without checking with me?"

Larsson's eyes narrowed. "First off, I don't check with you to do anything, Ranger. I'm so far above your paygrade you'd get a nosebleed stepping into my office. Second, I'm in *the United States government's* park because a red tide is about to wash ashore, and frankly, DHS doubts you can handle the situation."

"There isn't a problem in my park I can't handle."

"DHS disagrees. Especially since two campers disappeared yesterday."

"They didn't disappear. And how do you—?"

"We're DHS. We know everything, including that tourists don't need to spend the day here breathing in toxic algae spores."

"Algae doesn't have spores."

"Whatever it has, it makes people sick."

"I'm radioing headquarters," Kathy said.

"Knock yourself out."

Larsson's attitude *really* pissed her off now. She went to the main office and raised Park Service Headquarters on the radio. She finally got through to Fran Nelson, the regional director.

"Fran, I've got someone out here from DHS telling me the park is closed."

"We just sent out a press release and updated the website to that effect. Sorry you were brought into the loop late, it's all very last minute, an Agent Larsson was in early this morning. NOAA had a red tide coming your way and we can't risk visitor exposure."

Kathy was shocked that such a bullying ass could be legitimate. "Wow. But it's not red tide season."

"Explain that to NOAA. And I'm told that you and Toland should minimize exposure. Stay indoors, away from the beach until NOAA gives the all clear. Do whatever the agent there recommends to stay safe. Headquarters out."

That exchange should have made her feel better. Everything Larsson had said had been confirmed. But while a red tide was tough on the marine environment, since she and Nathan didn't have any chronic respiratory problems, it likely wouldn't affect them. Getting instructions to stay inside made no sense at all. And it certainly wasn't enough of an emergency to close the park and put someone else in charge.

There were a lot of bizarre things happening, and in too short a time for her to sort them all out. But she had an awful feeling that they were all connected in the worst possible way.

CHAPTER 13

Kathy's ears perked at the growing whine of rotor blades out to the east.

The entire Dry Tortugas was restricted airspace. That helicopter could only be from the military or the Coast Guard. And she expected neither. She left the office and went to the fort's main gate.

A huge, dual-rotor CH-47 helicopter screamed in just off the water's surface. The military aircraft was painted an ominous matte-black. It stopped at the water's edge and dropped the big ramp at the aircraft's rear. A gray Zodiac inflatable boat with an outboard clamped to the stern slid out and hit the water with a splash. The helicopter hovered sideways across the shore and set down on the east beach.

Nathan joined her. "I didn't order any pizza delivery. Friends of yours?"

"I'm afraid they're friends of Larsson," Kathy said.

Three burly men in black fatigues jumped out, one black, two white. One of the white men had his hair up in a Samurai top-knot. He waded into the water and pulled the zodiac ashore. Others inside the helicopter passed several crates and duffel bags out to the other two men. The black man gave the pilot a thumbs-up. The helicopter rose and headed back east.

Larsson emerged from the powder magazine and jogged for the main gate. Kathy held out a hand to block his way.

"Who the hell are those three?"

Larsson slapped her hand away as he passed. "They're with DHS. Stay in the fort and don't interfere."

Kathy had to stop herself from grabbing the smaller man by the collar and yanking him back into the fort. Instead, she gave Nathan a hand signal to stay put and followed a dozen feet behind Larsson.

The three men began inspecting the contents of several crates. When she got closer to see details, it was clear that unless DHS had started hiring felons, these three were not DHS. The black-ops uniforms were the first hint. The biggest one with the top knot had a hint of Asian features that made his hairstyle more sumo-wrestler level menacing than hipster-stupid. The other two weren't quite as big, but still intimidating. The black man's skin was dark as obsidian, and he sported a shaved head and a full beard. The white man had his sandy hair in a more conventional military style, but a full-color tattoo of a rattlesnake coiled around his neck worked hard to offset any normalcy. The three all screamed of ex-military turned para-military. Pistols hung heavy from web belts around each one's waist.

She didn't need a private army setting up in her park. The man with the top knot turned around and caught sight of Kathy.

"What's she doing here?" he said to Larsson.

Larsson looked over his shoulder and stopped. "Damn it. What *are* you doing out here? Did you hear me say not to interfere?"

"I heard you and ignored you."

The other two men closed the lids of the crates they were shuffling through.

"What did you bring into my park?" Kathy stepped closer to the crates.

The big man raised his hand in front of her. It was her turn to slap someone's hand away. She struck him and suddenly she was staring down the very black barrel of his pistol.

"A few rules," the big man said. "First, steer clear of our equipment. Second, touch me again and I will put you down. Hard. Are we clear?"

There was a complete lack of emotion in his black eyes, just cold, reptilian resolution.

"My man Valadez there," Larsson said, "he isn't real touchy-feely. I'd give him some breathing room."

She raised her hands shoulder-high to calm the situation. "Everything's okay."

Valadez stepped forward and pressed the pistol barrel against her chest. He eased Kathy's sidearm from its holster. "You seem a little hot-headed. I'm going to hold onto this for both our sakes."

"What the hell?" Kathy turned to Larsson. "You can't do this. This is my park."

"It's our park for a while," Larsson said. "And these men are here for your protection."

"Protection from what?"

"I think you need to get back in the fort," Valadez said. The request sounded more like an order.

Kathy was outnumbered, and in the dark about whatever was going on here. She was steaming hot and ready to make a stand, but her best bet was to back off until the odds turned more in her favor. She turned and retreated to the fort. The empty holster beat against her leg with each step and kept her anger simmering. She passed through the gate. Nathan looked at her holster, confused.

"They took your pistol?"

"At gunpoint. Those three work for DHS about as much as I work public relations for Japanese whalers. Follow me."

She led him into the office and went to the radio. She flicked it on. It whined with static and an odd oscillating tone.

"And, ouch," Nathan said.

Kathy grabbed the mic and tried to raise Park Headquarters. All that answered was white noise.

Nathan went to the commercial radio and flipped on the Key West station. Nothing but the same static.

"Either we're the last survivors of the apocalypse..." Nathan said.

"...or all the radio signals are being jammed," Kathy finished.

CHAPTER 14

As soon as the park rangers disappeared into the fort, Charlie Valadez, the mercenary with the topknot, turned and lit into Larsson.

"Why were we sent out here early? We don't have all our gear. The emitters are still in Naples."

"A string of unfortunate circumstances accelerated the schedule. A second flight's coming with the rest of the gear, and it's swinging by Naples for the emitters."

Valadez bit his lower lip and grimaced. Experience said a lot was bound to go wrong during any mission. Starting out all screwed up was just tempting fate.

"First," Larsson said, "I need reconnaissance around these keys. Take someone with you. Confirm this place and the waters around it are empty."

Valadez bit back a sharp answer. "Roger that."

Larsson headed back to the fort. The other two mercenaries joined Valadez.

"What was with the big rush to get out here?" Zimmer, the sandy-haired man with the neck snake, said.

"Sale on crab salad," Wilson, the black man, answered.

Both of them laughed.

"Cut that short," Valadez said. "Our employer is a firm giant crab believer, so while we are getting paid by said employer, we are, too. Wilson, set up an overwatch at the fort entrance and keep the rangers in their cage."

"Aye, aye." Wilson had spent too much time in the Navy. He headed for the fort.

"Zimmer," Valadez said, "you and I are taking a boat ride."

"Boat ride?" Zimmer said. "Me? He's the former SEAL. Let him take the boat ride. I don't do the water."

"Can't swim?" Wilson said.

"And don't want to," Zimmer said. "You see any gills on me?"

Valadez went to the Zodiac and rotated the stern into deeper water. Zimmer grabbed an assault rifle from one of the crates, slapped home a magazine, and hopped into the bow. Valadez fired up the outboard and backed the boat away from the shore. With a twist of the throttle, he spun the Zodiac around and headed away from the key.

The water beneath the Zodiac had a turquoise tint and amazing clarity. In the shallows, individual shells and bits of coral were easy to see. The water remained clear even farther out, with coral reefs appearing as darker patches against the white sand.

Zimmer suddenly jumped from the port to the starboard side of the Zodiac. "Damn, did you see that?"

Valadez peered into the clear water. "See what?"

"A damn shark. Ten feet long if it was an inch." Zimmer tucked himself back into the bow.

"For the love of God," Valadez said. "You're in the boat, it's in the water. You're safe."

"I've seen *Jaws*. No one's safe."

Valadez was willing to do something to spice-up this useless recon, and shark-watching fit the bill. He rolled down the power and steered the Zodiac in a lazy left-hand circle.

"What the hell?" Zimmer said. "You trying to piss the thing off?"

Valadez caught sight of something long and dark down below. He cut the engine to idle. The Zodiac slowed and coasted over a shark on the sea floor about a dozen feet down.

Zimmer peered over the boat's side. "There! See. Damn monster shark."

"That's not even ten feet long. And look at its head. It's a nurse shark. You can practically sit on one and it won't care."

"Yeah, well, a shark is a shark. I say we finish this and get back to dry land."

Valadez opened up the engine and sent the Zodiac back on course around the key. "Why is it you took this island mission if you're so Chicken of the Sea?"

"My daughter wants a trip to Disney World for her birthday. And I'm not scared of the water. I just respect it."

"Chill out, Mr. Respect. People come out here to go snorkeling. Nothing is going to kill you."

The boat lurched up and down. Water rippled all around the sides. Something scraped along the length of the boat's carbon fiber bottom.

Suddenly, half of a giant, open crab claw burst up through the Zodiac's bottom. It severed Zimmer's left leg like a carving knife. The claw's other half broke the water's surface off the port side. Zimmer screamed as blood pumped out of the stump of his thigh.

The boat came to a dead stop, the engine screaming in protest. Valadez threw the prop in reverse. The Zodiac stretched against the immovable claw.

Then the claw snapped shut. The raft boomed as the claw popped an inflatable compartment. Fiber shredded as the claw sheared the raft's bottom.

A second claw swept in from the other side. It clamped tight around Zimmer's midsection. His scream went to a higher pitch and his wide, pleading eyes locked on Valadez's.

Then the claw pinched closed and dragged Zimmer underwater. Seawater surged into the bottom of the raft. Zimmer's rifle washed out into the Gulf.

If he tried to go forward, he'd scoop water straight in through the damaged bow and flounder the raft in an instant. Valadez twisted the throttle wide open in reverse. The Zodiac's twin tails smacked against the waves. Valadez gripped the motor housing with both hands and struggled to keep the raft pointed toward the key.

Beneath the boat, the sea floor changed color. Valadez glanced down. A giant crab skittered across the sand and coral, pacing the flooding raft. It had to be over twenty feet across. Seaweed and remora fish clung to its shell. Zimmer's limp corpse fluttered in its left claw. A red slipstream of blood painted the water in the body's wake.

Black eyestalks protruded from the crab's head. One faced forward. The other rotated and pointed its black eye up at Valadez.

The crab pulled ahead. The creature was going to cut him off from the beach. If it got the chance to punch through the Zodiac again, he was a goner.

Grey fins with black tips knifed the water on either side of the raft. Two reef sharks zipped past the raft like it was standing still. They dove along the dissipating blood trail, toward the crab.

Valadez cut the Zodiac right. The sharks accelerated through the clear water on a beeline for Zimmer's body in the crab's claw.

The crab spun around to face the predators. One shark darted out ahead of the other. The crab's eye stalks turned to the approaching fish. It crouched down in the sand and tucked Zimmer just under the front of its shell.

The sharks dove in formation, the second's nose just off the first's pectoral fin. Their tails swept the sea in rapid unison as the fish sprinted in to grab Zimmer's corpse.

One great claw swept up and crashed against the lead shark. It deflected the fish and the shark careened off to the left.

The turbulence slowed the second shark and doomed it. The crab's other claw darted out and snapped shut just behind the shark's dorsal fin. The powerful fish cleaved in two. Its eyes rolled up in its head. The tail drifted down to the seafloor. Momentum kept the front half of the shark going forward, but it slowed, rolled on its side, and bumped harmlessly against the crab's shell. The crab dropped both claws back down to protect Zimmer's body from the next attack.

Valadez's heart pounded in his chest. He angled the Zodiac back to the key. From behind, he watched the surviving reef shark make a second pass at the crab. But at the last moment it broke right, opted for an easier meal, and scooped the tail of its dead brother off the sand instead.

The shark attack was the delay Valadez needed. The Zodiac churned into shallow water off the south-facing beach. The prop bit into an outcrop of coral and the engine ground to a stop. Valadez jumped out into thigh-deep water and splashed ashore as fast as he could. He made the beach and turned back to see a claw clamp down on the drooping Zodiac and pull it away and under the surface. Muffled booms sounded under the water, and bubbles from the raft's burst compartments turned the surface white.

Valadez drew his pistol and pointed it at the sea. His chest heaved with huge breaths as he awaited the crab's final assault. The gun trembled in his hand.

But the sea went calm. The surface returned to a pattern of placid ripples that kissed the shore as tiny waves. A Caribbean postcard picture.

Valadez's heart slowed. He lowered his pistol and backed away from the shore. He turned to face the reddish hulk of Fort Jefferson and wondered if crabs could climb walls.

CHAPTER 15

Valadez's fear of the crab turned to fury over Larsson as he marched to the crates near the east beach. He pulled out a rifle, jammed in a magazine, and headed for the fort.

From the open main gate, Wilson watched him approach. He looked back at the east beach, as if maybe he'd missed the Zodiac's return, then back at Valadez. "Hey, Chief. What's going on? Where's the boat?"

"It's gone. Shredded by the biggest crab I've ever seen."

Wilson laughed. "Oh, yeah, good one." He studied Valadez's face. "Wait...you're seri—Where's Zimmer?"

"The crab killed him. Chopped him up and pulled him under. I barely got to shore."

"Damn, those things are real? How can that be?"

"I'm about to find out. Keep a watch for something big to come crawling out of the ocean." Then he pointed to the two park rangers standing by their quarters. "And make sure those two stay put."

"Aye, aye."

Valadez shouted at the two rangers. "You two get inside and stay there!"

The little nerdy one looked scared and scampered inside one of the rooms. The tall woman he'd disarmed shot him a pissed off look before backing in. As he'd thought from the start, she was going to be a problem.

Valadez went straight to the powder magazine. Inside, electric lights lit up a variety of historical displays along the walls. Larsson sat at a wooden table, tapping on a laptop. He looked at Valadez's disheveled appearance with concern.

"What the hell happened to you?" he said.

"Zimmer's dead. The Zodiac's gone. A giant crab tore the crap out of both of them."

"Damn it, I told you not to engage those things."

"It engaged *us*. And I can tell you right now that we don't have the firepower now to take something like that out."

"The CH-47 is making a second trip with the rest of our gear, including the big Zodiac. Then you'll have everything you need and more."

Valadez sagged against the wall from a combination of exhaustion and frustration.

"Oh, I see," Larsson said. "You thought I was crazy or full of bull. You didn't think there were giant crabs, and that you were going to just spend a week at the beach. Well, surprise. I wasn't lying."

"Where the hell did those things come from?"

"They've always been here, long before people I guess. The CIA found them, but they were only about half that size. A little chemical, genetic mutation for size and stronger shells and, poof, super crabs."

"What the hell for?"

"Foreign intervention with plausible deniability. A natural disaster that would wreak havoc on a country and couldn't be tied to the USA. Relax, the emitters will make this island the literal safest place in the world from giant crabs. And they'll be on their way to Cuba where they were always supposed to be."

"What support do we have if these things end up being more than we can handle?"

Larsson shook his head. "None, so they can't be. This little operation was off the books in 1961, and it's off the books now. The Agency wants this kept out of public consumption. I promised I could get this job done quietly with you contractors, and we'll do just that."

A voice crackled from Larsson's laptop. "Whiskey Two Four this is Tango Seven. We are inbound."

"There," Larsson said. "Second load of gear on the way. Just as planned. Get Wilson to the beach and guide in that slingload."

Valadez grabbed his rifle and headed for the fort's main gate. Wilson stood on the terreplein above him.

"Everything we need to blow those things to hell is on the way in," Valadez shouted up to him. "Come with me down to the beach."

"What about the rangers?"

Wilson had a point. They didn't need the two rangers added to a mix that had already started to sour. But now they were a man short.

"First things first. The sheep will stay in their pen for a while. If we don't get the rest of our gear, we may all end up being on the wrong end of a crab dinner."

CHAPTER 16

Larsson cursed and banged his hand against the wooden table. Without an audience, he could let his true emotions vent. How could this op get so screwed up so quickly? They'd just hit the beach.

Larsson's satellite phone rang. He uttered another low curse. It was Gil McCafferty, his boss at the CIA. There were days he wished he really did work for DHS instead of just using it as part of his cover. He picked up the phone.

"Larsson here."

"Great!" Gil's voice wasn't filled with happiness. It was more a mix of sarcasm and fury. "Why don't you tell me where the hell 'here' is?"

"At a lodge by the lake upstate."

"You need to get back to work. We've lost an asset."

"Really?"

"A surveillance trawler. Left Tampa without a mission, went dark, and disappeared."

Larsson feigned surprise at hearing about the hijacking his own crew had done. "Stolen?"

"No one steals a CIA ship without knowing what it is, and how to get to it. Sounds like an inside job."

"Do we have suspects?"

"Not yet. We're pulling background and recent comm. There are related security breaches, missing funds. The whole thing's a mess and you need to get in here to help get to the bottom of it. You've worked the South Florida area."

"No problem. I'll pack it up and be in tomorrow morning."

McCafferty hung up.

Larsson jumped up and threw the chair across the room. This whole plan had gone sideways from the start. He'd lost contact with his team that stole the trawler after the helicopter had picked up the repaired emitters. They should have been back on the mainland, setting the ones closest to the Naples shoreline. Had the ship had mechanical problems? Had some kind of Coast Guard presence sent them off in a different direction? He hoped they survived. The people on it deserved to see the crabs wreak their revenge. Despite the cover story he'd fed Valadez and his trained monkeys, the crab's target wouldn't be Cuba. It would be Naples and the U.S. mainland.

He had to have faith that this was how justice worked. Inexorably moving in the direction of right, no matter the obstacles that popped up in its way. After the Bay of Pigs failure, his CIA agent father had been double-crossed and abandoned behind the Iron Curtain. Larsson had spent his career plotting his revenge, recruiting the other disaffected, making the contacts he'd need to bring the CIA's creations back to America, to make certain those metaphorical chickens came home to roost.

He imagined the horror in the CIA when the first realization hit, that the rampaging crabs were their creation. And just as the horror of having to explain that to the world seeped in, he'd announce to all that he was the one that made it happen, and that the CIA's own ills were the cause of the destruction the crabs created.

Would the nation hail him as a hero whistleblower? Probably not. They'd contend that he could have exposed the truth without all the carnage and destruction. But who listens to the subtle voice in the wilderness anymore? Who would keep the government from covering up everything again, as they had for decades? No, this way, his way, was the only way. No matter how he might be condemned now, history would praise him as a hero who brought evil to light and vindication for his father.

Today's bright spot was that no matter what, he knew Gianna Madera wasn't still alive. She'd pissed him off from the first moment he'd kidnapped her. His team had orders to kill her as soon as she'd used her expertise to repair the emitters. Since she'd completed the only unfinished task that had kept her alive, she had to be dead. When the CH-47 finished unloading, he'd have the sonic emitters, and be able to start leading these crabs to a feast.

But he'd need to hurry. By the time he didn't show up for work tomorrow, the Agency would know what files were breached, that the missing money had bought helicopter sorties in the Florida Keys, that he'd fed the NPS a load of bull about a red tide, and that the people who hijacked the trawler had been communicating with him. Then it would all hit the fan. The Agency would terminate his rogue op, and with extreme prejudice.

CHAPTER 17

Nathan stood at the window of his quarters. Kathy sat in a chair. He'd watched Valadez, soaking wet and pissed off, march into Larsson's office, then leave and take Wilson with him. Both had been armed with assault rifles.

"The Band of Bummers out there are short one and armed for World War III," Nathan said. "Something about their plan has gone awesomely wrong,"

"And that plan doesn't have a damn thing to do with any red tide," Kathy said.

She noticed an oil lamp on his desk. "You knew we had electricity when you packed to come here, right?"

Nathan looked over. "Oh, that's for moments of period accuracy. A little lamp light like they did in the 1860s."

"Can you see with that?"

"Hardly at all. That's why people used to go to bed when it got dark."

Nathan looked back out the window. The door to the powder magazine reopened. Larsson stepped out with a backpack over one shoulder and a map in the other. He ran over to the ranger's office

"Larsson just entered the main office," Nathan said. "And our guard along the wall has headed for the beach."

"They underestimate us rangers. We can work that to our advantage." Kathy stood up and went to the door. "Now's our chance to find out more about his plan. I'm going to check out the powder magazine. He picked that place for a reason."

"I doubt he left you a war wall with cut-out pictures and red strings on pins."

"But he might have left something."

"Dude seems to have anger issues. Probably best he doesn't catch you in there."

"I'll be in and out. But if he does, I'll say I was moving some of the artifacts out for their safety."

"I'll sneak over to the dock," Nathan said. "See if I can hide the skiff under the dock house. They don't need to know we have it."

"We'll have one chance to get away with something before Larsson realizes we're a threat. Avoid the main gate and duck out through a gap in the cistern passage in the south bastion. No one at the beach will see you come and go. The moat looks deep, but sand and some old stonework provide a calf-deep passage to the campground."

"Every moat's Achilles's heel. Sediment."

Nathan left his quarters first and darted into the structure of the fort. He stuck to the shadows and made it to the south bastion. Crumbled brick had left a slit about a foot and a half wide in the wall. Kathy was right. Just under the murkier moat water, he could make out a sandy path to the campground area on the other side. He hopped out into the burning sun, stepped into the warm, stagnant water, and waded across. He looked over to the beach where the helicopter had landed. The two men were engrossed in the crates. He still crouched as he sloshed through the water. He stepped out on the other side and shook some of the water from his shoes. He dashed across the sand, past a small stand of trees in the empty camping area, and over to the dock.

Kathy had left the skiff beached in the lee of the boathouse. There was no way Larsson had seen it when he'd disembarked. Nathan grabbed the bow and pushed the boat's stern into the water. He waded in after it. Ducking, he stepped into the dusky gloom under the planking. The smell of algae with a trace of dead fish hung in the confined space. Using a line tied to the bow, he pulled the little boat under the dock and tied it off to a piling in the middle. Larsson wouldn't see it unless he hung his head over the side of the dock and squinted.

Nathan checked the high water mark along the pilings where the barnacles stopped. When the tide came in, it looked like the boat would still have clearance. Barely. He'd hate to explain to Kathy how he'd gotten the thing crushed.

He left the boat and waded back out of the water. He peered around the corner of the dock house. The mercenary crew was still busy at the east beach. He jogged through the campground and past the trashcans and trees.

Something rustled in the trees.

He froze. There wasn't any wildlife on the island big enough to make that noise. He waited for the third mercenary to step out, gun drawn.

Instead, he saw a woman's face.

CHAPTER 18

Kathy left Nathan's quarters moments after he did. She sprinted across the courtyard, entered the powder magazine, and closed the door behind her. Originally, the separate, windowless building had been where the soldiers had stored the explosive gunpowder. The Park Service had restored it as a museum for Civil War artifacts.

She clicked on the lights. The park ranger in her could not help but look for any damage Larsson might have done to the displays. But everything was in its place and unmolested, save that the central table had been moved over a few feet.

Nathan was right about one thing. Larsson hadn't left anything around that might explain what this gang was really doing here. In fact, he'd left nothing. Whatever Larsson had, he must have stuffed in his backpack.

She looked down and realized that the floor didn't look right.

White sand filled the maze of joints between the bricks. She'd tried so many times to sweep it out and found the effort futile. But the spot usually under the table didn't look like the rest. An outline around one rectangle of bricks contained no sand.

She dropped to her knees and ran a finger along the clean line. A crack ran between the bricks.

She pushed the table to the side. She traced the crack's outline and discovered a loose brick. She pried it up. It was only a quarter-inch thick. Instead of earth underneath, there was an oak panel, with an iron pull ring. Kathy yanked at the ring and the entire section of bricks she'd been inspecting rose on a hinge. A musty, damp smell wafted up from the space below. Every brick in the trap door was only a quarter inch thick and secured to the inch-thick panel that made the trap door.

Kathy had seen construction plans for the fort. The foundation ran deep under the magazine to keep the whole place from sinking into the sand, but nowhere did they even hint that the magazine had a basement.

Kathy pulled a penlight from her belt and peered into the hole. Concrete steps descended into a room below. The concrete was an anachronism, a recent grade that would not have been available to the brick masons building the fort. Nathan would be beside himself with the historical impact of her discovery.

She descended the stairs. The walls were concrete block, gray, and low quality. Cracked and crumbled joint mortar and poorly aligned blocks testified to slipshod, rapid construction work. She wondered how it could have been done at all with Park Service personnel on site.

She eased her way down the stairs. They stopped in the middle of a good-sized room. She played the penlight's beam across a collection of dusty, obsolete technology. Reel-to-reel tape recorders. Bulky mechanical adding machines. Slide rules and pencils. Radios with mics bigger than her hand. Heavy, black rotary phones. She picked one up in the vain hope of a dial tone. It only offered silence.

Ceramic coffee mugs sat beside a steel electric percolator with an open, rusting can of Maxwell House beside it. Kathy looked inside. In the dampness, the contents had solidified into a termite mound of grounds. Whoever had been running this little post had left in a hurry, or stepped out thinking they'd be right back.

A new nautical map had been duct taped to the wall. A location southeast of Bush Key in open water had been marked with a circle in red pen. Several other points between there and Naples were marked with small green stars.

On a table to the left sat a series of binders. Kathy flipped one open. The cover page was labeled Top Secret and emblazoned with the logo of the Central Intelligence Agency. She turned the page.

Dense printing listed descriptions of the radiological and chemical mutations effected on a species of giant crabs. The date on the document was 1961.

"Oh my God," she whispered.

The crazy story from the old man in the cabin cruiser wasn't so crazy after all. The CIA had somehow crudely bio-engineered the crabs that Marc had described. She flipped through a few more pages. They contained the attack plans on the island of Cuba.

Nathan needed to see this. This book was historian's gold.

But first, she needed to get the hell out of here. Larsson catching her here would be beyond bad. She needed to get this back to Nathan, so they could both study exactly what the CIA had tried to let loose in the Caribbean.

She slammed the book shut and headed for the steps. She climbed the first two, looked up, and froze.

Larsson stood at the top of the steps. He pointed a pistol at Kathy's chest.

"What the hell are you doing in here?" he said.

"Discovering some truths about what's going on."

"Looks like you'll need to keep those truths to yourself," Larsson said. "I'd kill you now, but you might come in handy later. I can wait."

He reached up and dropped down the trap door. It landed with a heavy thud and the basement plunged into darkness. Something heavy scraped across the floor above her. Kathy scrambled up the steps and tried to raise the trap door. It didn't budge.

She collapsed on the steps. Larsson had her trapped in a place Nathan didn't even know existed. With the concrete walls and the powder magazine's brick floor over her head, she could set off a bomb and Nathan wouldn't hear it. And even if Larsson didn't kill her, what if he completed whatever mission he was on and just never told anyone she was here?

The specter of slowly starving to death under Fort Jefferson made her shiver.

CHAPTER 19

The poor woman peering at Nathan from out of the campground trees looked a mess. She was Hispanic and thin, with a model's high cheekbones. Her matted, sand-flecked hair and tired, puffy eyes said that she'd spent the night out here. The terrified look on her face shifted to relief. She staggered out. Salt stains mottled her jeans and shirt.

"A ranger," she said. "Thank God. Please help me."

"Sure, no worries. We didn't think there was anyone on the key."

"My boat sank. I swam ashore." She looked east. "You have to hide me."

"Hide you from who?"

"Valadez and the others. The ones who went around the key in the Zodiac."

"You know them?"

Her eyes widened in panic. "Oh, God! You're with them."

"No, no. They've taken over the park. We don't even know why."

She wrung her hands together. "Please, just get me someplace safe."

Nathan considered hiding with her in one of the small structures on the dock, but Kathy, and Larsson for that matter, would be looking for Nathan in the fort. He needed to go back and this woman didn't look like she needed to be left alone right now.

"Come on, follow me," he said.

He led her back across the campground, across the sandbar bridge, and into the fort. A quick look across the courtyard confirmed it remained deserted. The guard also hadn't returned to the terreplein.

"It's cool. C'mon." Nathan led the woman to his apartment. Kathy hadn't returned yet. He ushered the woman in, then pulled the curtains. She collapsed into a chair and exhaled an exhausted sigh.

"I'm Nathan. What's your name?"

"Gianna Madera. I work at Silenius Imports. Sonic research. I have a million confidentiality agreements I'm breaking by telling you this, but you're technically a government official, and besides, once I'd been kidnapped, all bets were off as far as I'm concerned."

"Why does an import business need a sonic researcher?"

"I didn't work in the 'above ground' part of the business. I did covert work in the basement, black ops projects for the government. I'm not even sure which government department. Sonic research is cutting edge. You wouldn't believe the weaponry on the drawing board."

"And you were kidnapped?"

"Yeah, Larsson and that thug in the Zodiac, Valadez. They broke into my apartment in the middle of the night, injected me with something, and the next thing I know they're unzipping me from a body bag on a fishing trawler. Only no one was fishing off this boat. There were nets on the deck, but the hold was full of electronics they put me to work on."

"Were they weapons?"

"No, and they weren't anything we created at Silenius. They were too old. Some kind of sonic devices. The tech was like Apollo-moon-mission stuff. I upgraded it with new tech they provided. The final acoustic bandwidth was real tight, the hydrophone transducer was state of the art, untethered with a wicked high PPS."

"I'll pretend I know what you're talking about. What were these devices listening for?"

"They didn't listen, they transmitted, sending one specific signal with an underwater range of about fifteen miles, but real strong if you were right on top of it."

"What would they sound like?"

"To us? Nothing. I don't even know what, if anything, could hear it. I'm an engineer, not a biologist."

"So how did you get to the fort?"

"I used the tech I had available against them. I disabled the trawler, then set a sonic charge against a weak part of the hull. I vibrated a drive shaft so hard it cracked a hole in the boat and down it went. I made it to the deck and escaped in one of the kayaks they used to put the emitters out for testing."

"Wait. The boat you swam away from wasn't the trawler, it was a kayak? The yellow one that sank in the storm?"

"That was me."

Nathan sighed with relief. "Awesome! We thought you'd drowned. Kathy, she's the other ranger here, will be psyched. She tried to rescue you in our skiff."

"I saw her coming. But I didn't know where I was, if she was someone I could trust. I hid in an air pocket under part of the kayak and swam it ashore."

"You were still lucky. That was a rough storm, strong enough to snap that kayak."

"The storm didn't do that. Something else did. I mean, the wind was whipping rain and seawater in my face, and the waves were pretty tall, but something else sliced that boat in half. I didn't get much of a look at it, since it was a few inches from my face, but it was like a big pair of scissors came up on both sides of the boat, snapped shut, and cut it in two. If I hadn't been kneeling, it would have severed my legs."

The first thing Nathan's mind went to were the crab stories from the old man in the cabin cruiser, but no way was that possible.

"So if that trawler sank, whatever you were working on sank with it."

"No, there was a helicopter there before the boat sank. It retrieved the emitters. The only reason I got away was because the crew had abandoned ship."

From outside came the sound of a helicopter.

"Damn," Nathan said. "The last thing we need are more reinforcements for these fake DHS agents. I'm going to stick my head outside the fort and see what's going on. Stay here and stay out of sight. You can change out of those clothes into anything of mine you can find that fits. Lock the door. Don't open it for anyone else."

"No problem there. And thank you." She gave him a brief hug. "I was sure I was about to die a dozen times in the last day."

"Well, Kathy and I will keep you alive. I mean, what's safer than a military fort, right?"

She managed a small smile. He declared that a victory and headed out. She locked the door behind him.

Nathan went to the second level of the bastion. He knelt in the shadows and looked through an embrasure to the east beach. Valadez and the bald black man were near the crates dropped off that morning. Larsson was nowhere to be seen. In the distance, he saw the big twin-rotor helicopter approaching for a second delivery.

He lit a flicker of wishful thinking that perhaps the helicopter was coming to take the island's unwelcome visitors away. Reality snuffed the flame.

CHAPTER 20

Valadez and Wilson stood by the crates of supplies at the beach. Rotors pounded the air in the distance. The speck of the CH-47 appeared, and then grew as it closed on the key. Underneath, an oversized pallet hung from four cargo straps. Crates filled the pallet.

"Well, that's a welcome sight," Wilson said.

"All the firepower we need for a dinner of cracked crab," Valadez said.

He moved to where the helicopter had landed earlier. From there, he and Wilson wouldn't have to drag the Zodiac very far to get it to the water.

The helicopter came in low over the sea, under any area radar. The pallet skimmed the wave tops. Valadez slung his rifle across his back and raised both hands over his head in the military signal for "assume guidance." The helicopter's landing light flashed in acknowledgment. It slowed and angled for Valadez.

"How much butter you think we'd need to eat a crab that big?" Wilson said. "I'm thinking fifty-five-gallon drum."

The helicopter closed to within a hundred yards of the beach. Two pilots in flight helmets with smoked visors stared out from the outer two of the cockpit's three windows. One pilot cracked a wide smile. Valadez waved the aircraft forward.

Two huge claws burst from the water on either side of the pallet. They clamped onto the front cargo straps and pulled.

The pallet dove into the sea. The helicopter jerked down and sideways. Engines screamed as the pilots fought to regain control. They brought the helicopter level, but then two more claws surfaced and grabbed the other two cargo straps. The pallet plunged beneath the waves and pulled the helicopter sideways after it.

The rotors struck the water first. The aircraft shuddered as the blades shattered into a thousand pieces. Then the fuselage slammed into the water.

Cold water hit superheated alloys and the turbine engines exploded with two ear-splitting booms. Then a deeper, louder explosion came from underwater. The earth shook under Valadez's feet. A mushroom of white water rose ten meters in the air where the chopper had gone down. Chunks of metal rocketed out in all directions.

Valadez and Wilson hit the sand and covered their heads. Debris rained all around them. A shard of sharp steel grazed Valadez's leg and left a hot slice in its trail.

When the hail from Hell stopped, Valadez checked his leg. A gash ran down his thigh. Seeping blood, not shooting. He'd seen worse. Hell, he'd had worse. He pressed his hand against the wound.

"You okay, Chief?" Wilson said.

"Yeah." Valadez winced as the pain caught up with him. "It's nothing."

"So's all our demolitions."

Valadez looked out at the water, now so calm you could have thought that nothing had happened. The wrecked helicopter lay at an angle in several feet of water.

He hoped Larsson had a Plan B.

***

Nathan stared, dumbfounded at what he'd just witnessed from the embrasure. A giant crab had just destroyed a helicopter. Gianna's story made complete sense, and the old man in the cabin cruiser knew what he was talking about. Beneath Nathan, Larsson ran out of the main gate toward the crash site. Nathan saw his chance to get back to his apartment undetected.

He raced down the stairs and first stopped at Kathy's. Was she ever going to be shocked to see that the Cuban Crab Invasion tale was true. He pounded and called. No answer. Worry blotted out his excitement. She should have been back by now.

He hurried to his own apartment before Larsson or any of the others returned. He entered using his key and saw Gianna had showered and changed into a pair of his cargo shorts and a souvenir Dry Tortugas

National Park T-shirt Nathan was going to send back to his parents. She lay asleep on his bed. He wondered if until now she'd slept at all since the trawler sank two days ago.

Some of the inconsistencies he'd uncovered in the fort's history began to fit together. What he'd first blamed on pirates, could it really have been...?

He looked out his window. Larsson and Valadez were closing and barring the main gate doors. He opened his laptop and pulled up his history database.

Giant crabs changed everything.

CHAPTER 21

The first rays of sunlight to cross the terreplein came through the window and warmed Nathan awake. He'd fallen asleep on the floor sometime late last night in the midst of his research. He rolled over and looked to his bed. Gianna sat upright and looked down at him.

"I didn't want to wake you up," she said.

Nathan sat up and stretched. "I thought the same thing about you yesterday evening."

"Sorry, once I was clean, dry, and safe, I collapsed." She patted the chest of her souvenir T-shirt. "And I appreciate the clothes. But one question…"

She went to his closet and pulled out a pair of gray, woolen Civil War drawers. "What are these."

Nathan's face went red with embarrassment. He jumped to his feet, dashed over, and grabbed the shorts. He wadded them in a ball.

"Whoa, hey, uh, it's a thing I do. Little experiments in period living. That's Civil War-era underwear."

"Seems uncomfortable."

"So I found." He shoved the underwear under his mattress. "You missed the afternoon excitement. You won't believe it, but a giant crab attacked Larsson's men."

"What? How giant?"

"Giant enough to pull a helicopter out of the sky off the east beach."

"That's crazy."

"Totally unreal. But Kathy had an old man on a boat tell her a story about a CIA plot to use giant crabs as part of the Bay of Pigs invasion. We both thought he was whacked, but now…"

"Maybe my kidnapping does make sense. That explains why I was building underwater sonic emitters for these people. Maybe some kind of crab defense?"

"Given the caliber of Larsson and his goons, no way you were making something defensive. They wouldn't have to hide in the shadows if they were doing that. The whole thing prompted me to do more research last night, and this fort gets totally weirder with everything I read."

"Because it was built in the middle of the ocean?"

"For starters. And that it was armed with four hundred and fifty heavy naval guns. Fort Sumter, defending Charleston Harbor, was only designed for one hundred and thirty guns. Fort McHenry defended the city of Baltimore with only fifty. This place being slammed full of cannons makes no military sense."

"That *is* strange."

"Then there's the staffing. Initially, a military artillery unit was assigned here, but not their doctor. That dude was reassigned, and the first doctor was Joseph Basset Holder. But he was a doctor in name only, not a general practitioner, but a scientist. He arrived before the Civil War. And while other units rotated through during the war, he stayed until the war ended. On this miserable flyspeck of an island. When he finally left, he didn't continue in a medical practice. He ended up at the American Museum of Natural History in Washington, D.C."

Nathan stood and paced the room.

"So you want to know my theory? The Army sent a scientist to do science. And he was here doing science on giant crabs. And the guns weren't here to keep pirate ships at bay. They were here to keep crabs in the sea."

"If I'd heard a park ranger tell me that story last week," Gianna said, "I would have said he'd spent too much time watching monster movies. But with crabs attacking helicopters outside the walls, I'm a lot less skeptical."

"The fort design validates it even further. The place has a moat. The fort practically covers the key and already has the Gulf of Mexico as a moat. Moats are built to keep enemy soldiers from scaling the walls. These moats were built to keep crabs at a distance and under the cannon barrels.

"And one prisoner here, Dr. Samuel Mudd, even reported that he'd seen giant crabs. His stories were totally dismissed as lunatic rantings, but now, you know, maybe not. Then add in that casualty reports from the fort are sky high in that time period after the Civil War, all attributed to yellow fever. How do you get yellow fever?"

Gianna thought for a moment. "Mosquitos?"

"Nailed it! And where do mosquitoes breed?"

"Standing fresh water."

"Where in the hell is there standing fresh water on this sand bar?"

Gianna raised an eyebrow. "So you think yellow fever was some code for crab casualties?"

"You bet it was. And there's more. You saw all the rotting pilings and concrete ruins where you came ashore?"

"Sure."

"The site was nominally a coaling station for naval ships. Those are the remains of the docks and bins. But would you risk bringing ships to a site filled with prisoners and ravaged by yellow fever? No. That's why they didn't. The dock records show no coal deliveries ever made, and no ships ever arrived for coal. It was all a cover story."

"But to keep such a secret for so many decades..."

"There was no internet, no radio, not even national newspapers. It was much easier to keep things quiet back then. But not by the start of the 20th century. And that's where one more coincidence comes to light. And in history, there are no coincidences.

"There was a record of one ship coming here for a coaling stop. The battleship *U.S.S. Maine* in February 1898. Then it steamed into Havana harbor in Cuba and blew up. I'm going to guess that she came here to suppress a crab attack. Why else have the nation's newest battleship coal here when other stations were along the route to Cuba? Did damage in a battle with crabs later doom her, or did a crab hitch a ride on, or in, the hull to Cuba? I don't know what sank her, but somehow, neither did several boards of inquiry. Each came to differing conclusions."

"I'd call that a conspiracy-theory-stretch," Gianna said. "If it wasn't for the giant crabs outside."

Someone banged on the door. "Toland, get out here!" Larsson bellowed.

Nathan motioned for Gianna to get in the closet. She zipped in and closed the door behind her. Nathan opened the main door. Larsson looked tired and angry. He held a pistol in his hand.

"Who were you talking to?" he said.

"Huh? Oh, myself. Talking through a history hypothesis."

"You sounded ridiculous."

"That's why I don't listen when I do it."

Larsson squeezed the grip of his pistol, irked. "Come on. Work to do."

Nathan stepped out and shut the door behind him. He looked around. He didn't see Kathy and realized she'd never checked in with him last night. "Where's Kathy?"

"Out of the picture."

"Whoa, what does that mean?"

"It means you need to forget about her and do what I'm telling you to."

Nathan's heart sank as he imagined the worst. "If you hurt her—"

"You'll do nothing, because we have the guns and you have a park ranger badge." He poked the pistol into Nathan's ribs so hard that Nathan groaned. "Now get to the beach and help salvage some cargo."

"Out in the water? With the crabs?"

Larsson's brow knit. "You saw that?"

"Who could miss it?"

"Then yeah, you're going in the water with the crabs. Right alongside me and Valadez and Wilson. And everything you pull out just might save your life against those crabs, so slacking off might get you killed by something bigger than this." He gave Nathan another jab with the pistol.

The last thing Nathan wanted was to do a little personal combat with a giant crab. But he also wanted to redirect Larsson from the ranger quarters as quickly as he could, before Larsson decided he needed to wander around in there and check the closet. Nathan headed for the main gate. One of the doors had been reopened.

On the way, he passed several military-style crates on the parade ground that someone had already repositioned into the fort. One had a marking for 5.56 mm ammunition. Another had a stencil reading "Hand Grenades, M67."

He wondered if any of that would be effective against the biggest crabs in the world. In 1898, the Navy had sent a battleship.

CHAPTER 22

Kathy's watch indicated it was past dawn.

She'd never have known. The windowless former hideout for the CIA was like an isolation tank. No light, and with the thick walls, no sound. Even when she'd climbed the stairs and sat under the trap door, she'd heard nothing, though whether that was because the door was solid or because the powder magazine was empty, she could not tell. Every time the situation reminded her of a pharaoh's tomb, she tried hard to press the similarities back into her subconscious.

After the first half-hour of searching the room with her penlight, she'd stopped to conserve the battery. It was hard to not feel hopeless. The room had no power to get any of the archaic communication technology up and running, and she doubted that anything relying on vacuum tubes would still work anyway. The concrete block walls were shoddy, but they were sturdy. She wasn't going to chip through one and then dig herself out like in some POW escape movie. And Nathan wasn't going to find her. He didn't know this room existed and could look straight at the trap door and not see it. Hell, she had for over a year.

She might have slept some through the night; it was hard to tell. If she had, it was more fits of being overcome by exhaustion than restful sleep. Anxiety had kept her mind racing and by now the humid air had grown increasingly stale.

A realization dawned on her. Between heated vacuum tubes and human respiration, this room would have needed ventilation, and a lot of it. But she hadn't seen a vent.

She jumped to her feet and snapped on her flashlight. A quick play around the walls revealed only one thing hanging there, the new nautical map that Larsson had duct taped to the concrete. She pulled it down and revealed a rusting three-by-two foot air vent. She raised her palm against it and a faint puff of air tickled her fingertips.

The vent hung loose in the mounts. She wedged her fingertips into the gap and pulled. The rusted heads of the retaining screws popped off and the cover fell away. She shined her flashlight inside.

A seemingly endless, rusting, rectangular shaft. Gauzy veils of spider webs hung like multiple sets of curtains. About as inviting as a haunted house.

But when she clicked off her flashlight, she saw confirmation the journey would be worth it. At the far end shone the unmistakable glow of daylight.

"Tetanus and spider venom," she muttered. "Every girl's dream come true."

She stepped up on the desk and went shoulders deep into the shaft. Claustrophobia had always been her weak point. If the room had felt like a tomb, this thing felt like a casket. Her shoulders touched the sides, but if she canted her body and stuck her arms out ahead of her, she could fit. There just wouldn't be room for the spiders.

She climbed in and began to inch her way forward in the darkness. The sides of the shaft were so close to her face that she could feel her breath reflected back with every exhalation. Each push forward draped another set of sticky spider webs across her head. Panic swelled as the certainty that the walls were closing in manifested. She could practically feel the shaft tighten around her chest and compress her lungs.

She paused, pushed the fear aside, concentrated on the ever-strengthening current of fresh air beckoning from further up the shaft, and then pushed on.

The shaft made a right angle turn upward just ahead. The smell of salt and the sea replaced the stink of rust and decay.

At the angle, she had to force herself forward and up. Her spine screamed in protest at the contortion. She scraped her face against the shaft and felt blood seep onto her cheek. She inched upward. Daylight beckoned.

Her hips wedged in the angle.

The flush of panic she'd felt earlier returned as a full-on rush. This would be worse than dying in the CIA dungeon. Trapped here starving while spiders and who knew what else crawled over her withering body.

Terror raced through her. Her feet flailed to find purchase in the shaft, but they just slipped against the surface. Her heart beat so hard it seemed to flex the shaft's confining walls. The daylight overhead mocked her from behind a set of bars. A few feet up, but impossibly far away.

Suddenly, the heel of her boot punched through the weakened steel. She wedged it in and thrust her body forward. Her hips squeezed so tight she thought she'd pop, and then they slipped past the corner.

Kathy half-stood in the vertical shaft, her height finally working to her advantage after nearly trapping her. She wrapped her hands around a set of corroded iron bars that forbid her from the sun and open space above. She flexed her knees and pushed.

The grating popped free. She tossed it aside and pulled herself out of the shaft. She gulped the blessed fresh air.

Kathy stood on the concrete slab from the old north coaling station, surrounded by piles of old barrels and the remains of earlier naval stations. What she'd assumed was a random refuse pile she could now see was carefully arranged to conceal this secret room's air vent. She imagined CIA operatives laying everything just-so, the final touches to their new, secret base.

Her problem of escape solved, the next challenge arose. What to do next? Nathan was still in the fort, she hoped, but she didn't trust Larsson as far as she could throw him. Nathan was probably thinking the worst had happened to her after she hadn't returned.

She ducked down behind the barrels, but still had a good view of the east beach. She could not believe what she saw. The big CH-47 helicopter from the day before lay on its side, half-submerged in the shallows. The CIA basement had been soundproof enough that she hadn't heard a helicopter crash? What else had she missed?

She moaned as she imagined the mess the wreck had to have made of the east beach area. Coral habitat and sea life crushed. Then God-knows-what fluids were leaking into the pristine waters. She was ready to wring Larsson's pudgy neck for bringing this disaster to her park.

Larsson appeared on the beach. He waded out to the wreck with an automatic rifle slung across his back. Another man passed him, carrying salvaged cargo back up to the beach. Amidst innocuous crates and boxes lay a pile of odd red and white canisters. Valadez, also toting a rifle, sorted through the items on the beach, selected some, and headed back to the fort with them.

She finally got a better look at the man carrying the crates from the crashed helicopter to the beach. Nathan. And the pained, wary look on his face said his labor was far from voluntary.

Kathy was tired, hungry, and pissed off. She couldn't get back to the fort without being seen. She sure as hell wasn't going back down the shaft. And in an hour or so, the tropical sun would be high enough that she'd be dealing with the full ravages of dehydration.

She leaned against an empty barrel and took in a deep breath of the sea air. The worst part was that the rest of the world didn't know anything was going wrong at Fort Jefferson.

CHAPTER 23

Two charred corpses stared out from the downed helicopter's three-windowed cockpit.

Their eyes seemed to follow Nathan with each trip he took. The chopper lay on its side in several feet of water. In the left window, one pilot's head was just above the surface and bobbed in the waves as if nodding, saying, "Sure, come on in, but I'm proof of what happens out here." The center window was just a web of glazed cracks. In the third window on the right, the other pilot hung from the shoulder strap seatbelts, lips curled back in a creepy rictus, hands still gripping the top of the windscreen, as if at any moment it was about to climb out laughing.

The slingload cargo had hit the water to the aircraft's left. Crates and containers had obliterated chunks of coral reef and Nathan cringed at the ecological damage done to the park. The rainbow-hued sheen of jet fuel in the water alone was poisoning who knows how many species as he waded through it. The cleanup would take forever.

That's if there was anyone around to do a cleanup. If giant crabs overran the key, he could see the country just abandoning it, or worse, nuking it to keep the species from ever making Florida. A mainland invasion would be a nightmare.

He sloshed back to where the cargo lay strewn on the seafloor. The closer crates had already been recovered. He took a deep breath and went underwater.

The crystal clear water made finding the crates easy. Some remained in the shallows, but a bunch of them had tumbled down into the old coaling station channel, too deep to free swim down to. The tail of the helicopter hung a few feet out over the abyss. He swam to an ammunition crate and swept away a few curious shrimp. He grabbed the rope handles, planted his feet, and pulled it up. He surfaced in the water neck-high, and it was an effort to walk the crate and himself back toward shore. When the water lowered to waist-deep, Larsson stopped him and took the crate. He had an M-4 slung across his shoulder upside down, and he dragged the end of a rope through the water.

"I got this one. We need the Zodiac. It's still inside the bird. The rear cargo door is open. Swim over, tie this rope to the bow, and push it out."

"You know there are crabs out there?"

"You know we have guns over here? Get going."

Nathan took the end of the rope. He waded out halfway around the helicopter, then the water became too deep. It was over fifty feet to the end of the aircraft. Covering that would create a lot of crab-attracting splashing. But Larsson had probably killed Kathy, and wouldn't hesitate to kill him as well. And if he died, there would be no one to keep Gianna hidden.

He pushed off of the coral and began a quiet sidestroke to the rear of the helicopter. He didn't look down, didn't want to see whatever might be going on there. Instead, he focused on the Phillips screw heads along the helicopter's underside, following the rows, little X by little X, until the aircraft ended. He pulled himself around the cargo door and swam inside, the rope trailing behind him.

The Zodiac floated in the canted cargo hold. This was a larger model than the other one, with a set of controls in the center and a windscreen. One drooping section had been deflated, but he assumed the crew on the shore had the expertise to repair the puncture. An outboard motor and gas can lie on the metal floor within.

He swam inside and climbed out of the water along the ribbing inside the cargo area. He worked his way forward. An unknown viscous fluid dripped from the ceiling. The sickly sweet smell of the burned pilots made his stomach roil. He got to the bow of the boat and tied off the rope. With a nudge, he angled the Zodiac toward the opening, and then gave it a shove. The boat floated out the rear of the helicopter. The rope at the bow snapped up and out of the water. From the other side, Larsson pulled the boat out of view.

Nathan climbed back to the tail of the helicopter. He paused at the end and stared down through the jet fuel sheen to the sea floor. Tempting whatever lay in wait down there was not high on his list of things to do.

But it was still higher than spending more time in a derelict helicopter with two reeking corpses. He lowered himself into the water.

Underneath him, something moved.

He looked down, but the rainbow haze from the jet fuel obscured his view. No question he'd felt something big move through the water. The current from its wake had pulled at his legs. He ducked his head under and opened his eyes.

The twin black eyes of a giant crab stared back at him from feet away.

Nathan screamed out a thundercloud of bubbles. He broke through the surface and scrambled backward into the helicopter. He grabbed a rib of the cargo area and pulled himself out of the water.

Two enormous claws erupted from the water on either side of the fuselage. The claws snapped together like a pair of vise grips. The tips pierced the helicopter's sides and punched a foot into the cargo area on either side of Nathan. He splashed forward toward the cockpit.

The crab pulled and the chopper slid backward toward the deeper channel. Aluminum groaned as the nose angled up. The aircraft slid down into the water.

Nathan clawed his way higher into the submerging helicopter. He advanced but the aircraft retreated faster. Water rose past Nathan's thighs to his waist. His head banged against one of the aluminum ribs. The chopper's skin grated along the edge of the coral reef and a shrill shriek echoed in the interior, as if the airship wailed a dying cry.

Nathan grabbed the top of one pilot's seat. The charred corpse fell back and its head slammed down on Nathan's hand. It felt like over-grilled chicken skin.

The helicopter sank faster. A combination of rising water and the sinking chopper pushed Nathan up between the pilots' seats and over the console. He slammed into the cracked middle windshield. Sunlight, oxygen, and life beckoned from the other side. Then the sea washed it away as the crab dragged the helicopter under.

Nathan sucked in a last deep breath from the dwindling air pocket against the window. He pounded his hands against the glass. Nothing. He looked around in panic for any kind of a tool.

A .38 revolver hung in the pilot's shoulder holster.

Nathan pulled the gun free and slammed it against the window. Once. Twice. All that earned were muted thuds. His lungs screamed to exhale, his heart pounded in overdrive. Outside, the surface world retreated to a dimming blur.

Nathan shoved the pistol's barrel against the glass and pulled the trigger. A flash of powder and a muffled thump. The window shattered.

Nathan pulled himself through the window frame. Broken glass raked his sides. He kicked and windmilled his way to daylight.

Like a breaching whale, he broke the surface and sucked in a great, deep breath of the sweet ocean air. He splashed forward a few more feet until he was over shallow coral again. His feet touched the reef. Nathan fought the water as he pumped his exhausted legs to the shore. At the water's edge, he collapsed on the sand.

From behind him came a powerful splash. He glanced over his shoulder in time to see the crab surface as it climbed up from the shallows. A new wave of panic spiked his adrenaline and he scrambled up the beach.

To his right, the Zodiac sat beached and loaded with a pyramid of red and white emitters. Larsson popped up from behind the pile with his rifle and opened fire on the crab.

Valadez and Wilson rolled out on either side of the stack of crates a few yards away. They opened fire. Automatic weapons barked and flames spit in the crab's direction. Rounds hit its shell and ricocheted off with no effect. The crab hissed and crawled forward.

Nathan sprang to his feet and ran for the stockpile of crates. Valadez and Wilson fired past him. Bullets whizzed by his head like furious hornets. He dove over the crates for the perceived safety of the other side. He landed face first in the hot sand.

Rifles fired all around him. He looked back to see three streams of bullets converge on the front of the crab's shell. The crab shuddered but did not stop. A cloud of spent gunpowder swept over Nathan and stung his eyes.

"Pull back!" Larsson cried.

He ran for the crates. Then the three began a fighting retreat to the fort, firing, then reloading and firing again. Nathan saw he was about to be left behind, jumped up, and sprinted between them for the fort's main gate.

The crab kept coming.

Valadez pulled a round grenade from a cargo pocket. He pulled the pin and pitched it at the crab. It struck the crab square between the eyestalks and bounced back. It hit the sand and exploded. The concussion rocked the crab up on its rear legs. The front claws waved in the air.

Then the crab dropped back down on all eights. It hissed and resumed its charge for the four men.

Nathan made it to the gate and looked back. Larsson and Valadez were close behind. But Wilson had fallen. He lay on the ground, with the crab bearing down on him fast.

Wilson rolled on his back. Feet away from him, the crab reared up. With one hand, Wilson aimed his rifle and emptied a magazine of rounds into the crab's underbelly.

They did nothing.

The crab cocked back one great claw and jabbed. The claw hit Wilson in the chest and drove straight through into the ground. A cloud of sand and blood burst into the air, and then Wilson lay still. The claw slurped as the crab pulled it free.

Valadez screamed an obscenity and hurled another grenade. It landed under the crab and exploded. The impact made the creature shudder. It steadied itself, then continued toward the fort.

Larsson dropped to a knee and aimed. "Concentrate fire on the right claw!"

He and Valadez laid twin streams of rounds at the joint in the crab's right claw. An awful cracking sound split the air, then the smaller, lower half of the claw swung down at an unnatural angle. The crab stopped and emitted a furious hiss. It tucked the claw closer to its body and backed away. The claw's lower half left a trail as it dragged through the sand. The crab backed down the beach, into the water, and submerged.

Larsson turned to Valadez. "Got to get the ammo into the fort."

They both ran forward, straight past Wilson's severed corpse without a second glance. Each grabbed an ammunition crate and ran back for the fort.

Nathan ducked inside the gate. As soon as the two men entered, he closed the two oak doors and dropped the cross member across them to secure the entrance.

For the first time, the fort engineer's design was about to be put to the test.

CHAPTER 24

Kathy looked across the key from her hiding place. She gripped the edge of the old metal drum so hard her fingers tingled.

She had first watched in anger as Larsson forced Nathan to pull supplies out of the downed helicopter. Then in horror and disbelief as a giant crab attacked the wreckage and pulled it under with Nathan inside. Then in relief when Nathan surfaced and crawled ashore. Until Nathan had disappeared safe behind the fort's oak doors, she'd scarcely taken a breath.

The crab had killed one of the mercenaries. The act sickened her, and while she wasn't overwhelmed with empathy, being a man down in this situation wasn't good. She'd seen Larsson and Valadez try and fail to keep the crab at bay with rifle fire and hand grenades. They'd only injured it. It might be back. And it might bring more.

"Of course there are more," the science major in her said to herself. It was a species. To survive, there had to be more. A lot more. Crabs laid thousands of eggs. She imagined a dozen of them crawling up onto the beach. Or worse, into Key West. Or still worse, into Miami.

And there was nothing she could do. She'd never get back into the fort undetected with everyone on guard against crabs. If Larsson saw her outside the CIA room, he'd shoot her on sight, furious she'd escaped and afraid she'd be a dangerous loose end. She had no way to warn anyone on the mainland, and seventy miles to Key West was one hell of a swim. Her only option was to sit here, bake in the sun, sweat, and die. She wouldn't even live long enough to starve to death.

"Hey, Ranger," someone said behind her.

She whirled to see Marc Metcalf crouched down among the debris. He had a sheet sewn into the back of his long sleeve shirt, the ends attached at the cuffs and at the hems of his shorts. The sheet had sand glued to it, like flexible sandpaper. He wore a hat also coated with sand and speckled with seashells. Kathy gave the getup a confused look.

"What are you doing here?" she whispered, as if the men in the fort could have heard her if she hadn't.

"Kinda looks like I'm saving your butt. My boat's out west. Might be a good idea if we went aboard."

"How?"

Marc pointed to the water at the north end of the coaling station ruins. She didn't see anything. Then she did. A rubber raft, painted in a mottled sea camouflage pattern of greens and blues. At a distance, it was damn near invisible. Marc's cabin cruiser sat anchored well off-shore beyond it.

"I paddled it ashore," Marc said. "Two of us can get back in half the time. Gotta get cracking, while they're still too scared to take their eyes off the beach."

Paddling across the Gulf of Mexico with an eccentric old man wasn't the best option, but her choices were very limited. "Let's go."

She followed Marc in a shuffling crouch, trying to remain a small target if Larsson or Valadez happened to look this way. She had a bad feeling that both men had the marksmanship to pick her off, even at this range.

The raft looked like another of Marc's Navy surplus purchases. Close up, the camouflage paint appeared hand-applied. They pulled the raft out into the water and climbed in. It was a tight fit for two and the raft rode low. Warm seawater sloshed around the raft floor.

"Don't you worry none," Marc said. "The raft's like me. Old but still serviceable." He handed Kathy a short paddle. "The tide's with us, gotta go."

Kathy glanced over her shoulder. No one stood on the terreplein with a rifle trained their way. Marc had been right; everyone was focused on the beach.

"You painted this raft yourself?" she said.

"Specifically to match these waters. When I'm poking around near places the government don't want poked, I don't want the satellites picking me up." He tapped his hat. "Same with the camouflage clothing. I can crawl across any beach I'm exploring, and I disappear to even the newest drones."

Kathy thought those statements would have sounded crazy-paranoid a few days ago. But one crab attack later, they just sounded wise. "Why were you on the key just now?"

"Nothing like a big helicopter crash to arouse my interest. I watched it fly in from my boat, then it looked like something pulled it right out of the sky. I know for a fact there's only one thing in these waters that can do that, so I had to get a closer look. I got halfway to shore and —*bam, bam, bam*— it sounds a scene out of *The Sands of Iwo Jima*. I was gonna turn it around, but I saw you hiding out and thought you might need a bit of rescuing."

"And you were right."

"Sounds like a lot of firepower on that beach for the NPS."

"Because it isn't us. A guy named Larsson arrived with three others in tow claiming to be with Homeland Security, spouting some nonsense about a red tide on the way. I could tell from the start the story was crap, especially when a helicopter dropped off a ton of weaponry."

They made it to Marc's boat and went aboard. He tied the raft off to the stern. Kathy decided there was no risk telling him the rest of her story, and in fact, Marc deserved the validation.

"I stumbled on a secret basement," she said, "excavated under the fort in the 1960s. It was full of old radio and recording tech, as well as a lot of binders of material from the CIA. Those binders backed up everything you told me about the giant crabs."

Marc flashed an excited grin. "Did ya take any of 'em?"

"I escaped through an air duct. I barely got myself out of there."

His face fell. "The torture's always that there's never any hard proof to take anywhere. Not for almost sixty years."

Kathy's face brightened. "Wait, I have this." She pulled the wadded-up map from her pocket and laid it out on the seat along the cockpit. "It was on the wall."

Marc pulled reading glasses from the cabin, perched them on the edge of his nose, and leaned over. His eyes went wide and he slapped his thigh.

"Well, I'll be hog-tied. This is what I'm talking about right here. You see that embossed CIA stamp, Top Secret printed along the edge. This here's the real McCoy."

He knelt down and pored over the map in detail. He smacked his finger down on the red circle marker east of Bush Key. "That's it! That's the Number Two thing I've been searching for, the entrance to the crab colony. I was looking too far east. That monster on the beach, it came right out of there."

"And I'm guessing there are more following behind it if someone pulled the cork."

"There'll be a gaggle of them."

Kathy started to tell him a group of crabs was called a cast, but this really wasn't the time. "We need to call for help. Do you have a marine radio?"

"You betcha."

Marc lowered himself down into the cabin. His hesitant steps brought out his age in a way Kathy hadn't seen when he'd been rowing. His energy level and clear mind masked the fact that Marc was an old man.

Below deck, he flipped on the radio. A blast of shrill static filled the cabin. He spun down the volume. "Sweet Lord!"

"Jamming," Kathy said. "Same thing that happened to the NPS radio at the fort."

"Sounds like what the Cubans do to U.S. radio stations, but much worse."

"It has to be something Larsson put in place. I'd hoped your boat would be out of range."

"No way to get help," Marc said. "So we're gonna need to stop these things on our own."

Kathy thought maybe Marc had experienced a break from reality after all. "One crab took out a helicopter, and a pack of heavily armed men could barely slow it down. I'm not sure what you, I, and a tired old pleasure boat are going to do."

"We're gonna start by keeping everything that hasn't escaped the crab den trapped in the crab den. And this map marks the one and only door."

"We don't have anything to seal an opening in the sea floor."

"Not now. But we will."

"How's that?"

"Because like I said, finding their lair was my Number Two mission. I've already accomplished my Number One mission. Last month, I found my PT boat. And PT 904 went down carrying just what we need to keep those crabs in their place."

CHAPTER 25

Nathan, Larsson, and Valadez leaned against the closed main doors of Fort Jefferson. As the adrenaline surge retreated, Nathan felt his legs grow weak. He slid down to the ground

"How long can those things stay out of the water?" Larsson said.

"Are you asking me?" Nathan said. "They're your crabs."

"You're the park ranger science geek."

"Actually, I'm the park ranger history geek."

"Fantastic. When I need to know what day Lincoln was assassinated, I'll ask you."

"April 14th, 1865," Nathan muttered. "For future reference."

Valadez slung his rifle over his shoulder. Sweat rolled down the sides of his round face. He took a deep breath and turned to Larsson. "You want to tell me what kind of crab can't be stopped with a hand grenade?"

"The kind that was designed to take on the Cuban military," Larsson said, "then inbred for fifty years."

"We're not armed to take something like that down. Our mission was a short-term defense of the key from any locals. You said the crabs wouldn't even be here."

"And they weren't supposed to be. They weren't even supposed to be free yet. But the old warning system tripped. I thought it was just some component gone bad, but a crab showed up here, and the whole schedule had to accelerate."

"Sounds like between that and the helicopter crash the mission is FUBAR."

"Hardly. It'll be easier without having to free the crabs. The lures are there on the beach. The controllers should be in one of the crates here. Even with one deflated compartment, the Zodiac is serviceable. We're good."

"Someone want to fill me in on who you all really are," Nathan said, "and what you're doing, which totally has nothing to do with red tide."

"No," Larsson said. "I'll just tell you we're with the CIA. The rest is on a need to know basis."

"Almost being killed by a giant crab rates 'need to know' in my book."

"But not in mine," Larsson said. "Keeping yourself useful will keep you from being at the wrong end of my pistol. Start by helping us keep this fort secure. What other ways are there in and out of here?"

Nathan thought the south bastion fissure he'd used to get to the campground would be best kept to himself. It was too small for one of the crabs to use anyway. "One door, we just blocked it. The nature of designing a fort. And the embrasures are reinforced and too small for a crab to get in."

"Embrasures?" asked Valadez.

"The big holes the cannons stick through," Nathan said.

"You trying to make me sound stupid?" Valadez said.

"Hardly trying at all, actually."

Larsson shoved a pistol against Nathan's chest. "Make yourself annoying enough and you can stay outside the walls and become a tragic footnote in this place's history."

The barrel nearly broke through Nathan's skin. He stepped back. "I'm okay relating history, not joining it."

"How's being trapped in this fort going to help us?" Valadez said.

"The crab has to cross the beach, and the moat, and then it stops at the wall," Larsson said. "With that delay, we could get enough lead into it to injure it, like the last one."

"Unless one comes up out of the sea on the other side," Valadez said.

"The water shallows very far out," Nathan said. "The crab would be out of the water early."

"You need to be up there on watch to the east," Larsson said to Valadez. "I need time to assemble the controllers for the lures. Then we get out to the Zodiac and get this thing done."

"Roger that," Valadez said.

"You go up with him, History Ranger. Take the west end of the fort. Do anything stupid, and if Valadez doesn't shoot you first, I will."

Nathan thought of Gianna, hiding in his room, unaware of the second crab attack. "I have binoculars in my quarters, let me get them."

Larsson mulled it for a second. He waved his pistol toward Nathan's quarters. "Fast. Do it."

Nathan jogged to his quarters and went inside. As soon as he closed the door, he said, "It's me, don't come out. Larsson may be right behind me."

"Is everything okay?" Gianna said from the closet.

"Not even close. A crab attacked and killed one of the men. We're holed up in the fort defended mostly by blind faith. Whatever their plan is, they think they can still complete it. Larsson claims they're with the CIA."

"They *were* with the CIA. I gathered that from overhearing the people on the trawler. They'd all been wronged by the Agency at some point. I sensed a major undercurrent of revenge."

"He called the red and white canisters on the beach lures."

"If the crabs can sense the sonic frequencies the way other creatures do, they'd work that way. And if revenge is the plan, they'll be using those lures to draw the crabs to the mainland."

"I have to pull guard duty. Stay here and hidden. Larsson killed Kathy. You sank his trawler so I don't doubt for a second he'd kill you as well. We'll figure out a way to stop them."

Nathan pulled his binoculars off a shelf and left the room. He practically bumped into Larsson outside the door. He slammed the door shut behind him.

"What took you so long?" Larsson said. "Get up there!"

Nathan sprinted for the nearby stairs, desperate to draw Larsson away from his room as soon as possible. Instead, Larsson opened the door and went in.

Nathan froze at the base of the steps. He imagined the horror of Larsson dragging Gianna out by her hair, or worse, just the sound of a gunshot from inside his quarters. He held his breath.

Larsson stepped out alone and slammed the door behind him. Nathan scrambled up the steps before Larsson could realize he was there.

At the terreplein, he looked over and saw Valadez, rifle at the ready, watching the east beach. Out to the west, a single boat cut a slow path through the sea, far off. He raised the binoculars for a closer look. It was Marc Metcalf's cabin cruiser, from what seemed like weeks ago. Two people stood in the cockpit. One little man at the wheel wore a wide-brimmed hat that obscured his face. But he recognized the other. Tall, with dark hair and an embarrassingly filthy NPS Ranger uniform.

Kathy wasn't dead after all.

CHAPTER 26

From Marc's boat, the fort was too far away for Kathy to make out any detail, especially with the sun in her face. The good news was that she'd seen Nathan get into the fort before the crab had killed one of Larsson's men. She hoped Larsson had the brains to see he was short-handed and decide to keep Nathan alive.

Then Kathy thought about how furious Larsson would be when he found she'd escaped. She prayed he wouldn't take that anger out on Nathan.

But these were things she could not control. But she could seal off any remaining crabs from the rest of the world. Then they would have time to warn the country about the ones that escaped.

Marc stood at the wheel to the right of the cabin door. The old boat still had classic round gauges for speed and temperature that rivaled fine clocks in quality. But newer readouts stared out from an opening hacked into the side of the console. Sonar, hydrophones, a few other items she didn't recognize. The map she'd stolen hung clamped to a chart clip. The compass read due west.

"How long did it take you to find your PT boat?" Kathy asked.

"Years. I couldn't start looking for a while, didn't have no boat. Then with it being a secret mission and all, didn't have any real records or a location fix. Hell, didn't have no satellite nav back then. So I had to go by memory as to where she went down. And believe it or not, from sea level, all of the Gulf of Mexico looks about the same."

"Since they were armed, I can't believe the government didn't salvage the boats."

"Can't salvage something unless you're prepared to admit it exists. And after the Bay of Pigs, weren't no one in a hurry to admit nothing existed…not our boats, and especially not giant crabs."

A while later, the GPS pinged and Marc throttled back the engine.

"Welcome to White Shoal, conveniently just off the edge of NOAA's nautical map 11420. A swell place to anchor boats on a secret mission. Or so thought the CIA."

Marc went up to the bow and lowered an anchor into the water. He played out a hundred feet of line and tied it off to a cleat. When he returned to the cockpit, he flipped on a display. A green line swept around a black sonar dial. As it crossed the lower third, a fuzzy green outline of a ship's hull appeared.

"And that there is PT 904," Marc said. "About forty feet down. Resting in peace, and in pieces."

"Forty feet? When you said we were salvaging something, I assumed the boat was washed up on a key somewhere. How are we going to get anything up from there?"

Marc held up a finger for her to wait, then he lowered himself a step at a time into the cabin. He returned with a scuba tank. He hoisted it up onto the deck. It landed with a clank.

"I'm going to swim down and pick us up a torpedo."

"Torpedo? No way! You aren't swimming down there..." Kathy trailed off before insulting him.

"'At my age?' Was that what you were gonna say? I still dive every week, thank you. I'm perfectly capable. Are you certified to dive?"

"Well, no."

"Then I guess that brings it back to me, don't it?"

He disappeared back down into the cabin. After a little banging and cursing, he reemerged wearing a black wetsuit, carrying swim fins and a mask. The suit was riven with cracks, and small, missing chunks dotted the seams. With only his wrinkled face sticking out of the hood, he reminded Kathy of a turtle without its shell. In the skin-tight suit, he looked even frailer.

Marc opened a locker on the back of the cockpit and pulled out two heavy canvas straps. He slipped the loops at each end over the hook on the winch's cable. With a grunt, he swung the winch arm out over the water. He pushed a red down button with the palm of his hand and the cable unwound. He released the button and the cable stopped.

"Now when I go in, you're gonna press that red button so I can play out enough cable to get the straps around the torpedo. Then I'll scrape the cable hard enough to make it sing. That's your cue to use that green button to haul us up."

"How safe is raising a fifty-year-old torpedo?"

"I'm hoping safe enough we can handle it, and unsafe enough we can kill crabs with it. It can't go off without ignition. I dropped a bunch in the Coast Guard, and I'm still alive."

"You dropped them?"

"Yeah, but I'm older and wiser now. Gonna carry this one like a baby." He looked down into the water. "But to be safe, you should stop the winch with the fish well under the hull. Just until I get a full inspection in the daylight."

Marc finished donning the rest of his gear, adjusted his regulator and mask, and then dropped backward over the side of the boat. His head popped up from the water, and he grabbed the canvas straps with one hand. He gave her the thumbs-up with the other.

Kathy took a deep breath and pressed the red button. Cable played out from the winch. Marc's head dipped below the surface and with a splash from his flippers, he headed down, pulling the cable behind him.

Dread coiled around Kathy's spine as the deeper water swallowed the old man. She had an awful premonition he'd never resurface.

CHAPTER 27

Larsson stood under the withering sun in the parade ground beside the supplies they'd salvaged from the wrecked chopper. He shielded his eyes and could see Valadez on the east side of the fort watching the beach and the Zodiac. Ranger Nathan was watching the west side. If both his other men were still alive, hell, if one of them were alive, he'd shoot Nathan off the terreplein right now and let him plop into the sea as crab food. But Nathan had to stay. Larsson needed every set of eyes he could get so the crabs didn't get the drop on him, and, if necessary, someone expendable to throw to the crabs to save himself and Valadez, in that order.

He pried the top off the crate from the trawler. Inside were the two controllers for the lures. He pulled out one of the metal briefcases and opened it. The lower half held all the controls. For something so important, the controls were deceptively simple. A row of switches across the top—one for each of the lures, and master on and off switches on the bottom. Throw the switch to turn on a lure and a light beside the switch turned green and said that the lure was transmitting. Turn them on in the right order and an army of crabs would follow from one to the next, all the way to south Florida.

He powered the unit up. It completed a self-diagnostic and showed no faults. Finally, something about this plan was going right. Now he just had to get this into the Zodiac with the lures, and he'd be ready to lay a trail of sonic breadcrumbs for the crabs now that they'd been released from their trap. A few lures had been damaged, but he still had enough to do the job.

He'd need the map from the CIA bunker, and that reminded him that he had the other park ranger locked away down there. She ought to be hungry, thirsty, and a lot more compliant by now. But then again, there wasn't any reason to keep her alive. She'd been a pain in the ass since he'd arrived. A pistol in the ribs would keep the history ranger in line. He wasn't sure anything would keep Kathy from being trouble.

He headed back to the powder magazine and went inside. He slid the table back and pulled out his gun. Like a weightlifter's clean jerk, he threw the heavy trap door open.

"Good morning, buttercup," he said.

No answer.

Maybe she'd passed out from dehydration. That would make this much easier. No chasing her around to kill her. He pulled a penlight from his cargo pocket and snapped it on.

Step by step, he crept down the stairway. At the base, he played the beam around the room. He knit his brow. She wasn't there. He swept the beam across the walls. The backup planning map was gone. And the rusting air vent cover that had been behind it was missing.

"Oh, hell no."

He went to the ventilation shaft. It was just big enough for someone to escape through. He flashed his light inside and could see where swaths of the sides had been brushed clean of dust and cobwebs. And there was only one someone who'd been down here to brush them.

He cursed and kicked the table leg. He didn't know where this shaft opened up, but he could see some dim light at the far end. Since Kathy wasn't wedged in it, she'd gotten through it. And she had to be somewhere on the island.

He laughed. That meant she wasn't in the fort. And she wasn't getting in under Valadez's watchful eye or through that closed main gate. He had the keys to the Zodiac's motor, and all the ammo and weapons were behind these brick walls. Which left her trapped and defenseless, with nowhere to hide in the company of giant crabs.

She'd just become the poster child for out-of-the-frying-pan-and-into-the-fire.

Larsson wouldn't get the satisfaction of killing her, but knowing a crab would be doing it made up for the loss.

CHAPTER 28

Nathan couldn't help but wonder how many soldiers across time had stood where he stood atop the western face of Fort Jefferson, watching for the approach of an enemy by sea. Likely some of them had also been on the lookout for giant crabs.

The Gulf of Mexico lay deceptively calm with just the slightest chop. But beneath the surface, did a giant crab lie in wait? Did a dozen? If an army of them advanced on the fort, there'd be no stopping them.

At the fort's base, the stagnant water in the moat rippled. A current picked up and the water began to move like a slow stream. The level dropped slightly.

That shouldn't have been happening. The moat waters couldn't pump themselves out. There was no place for the water to go.

Soon the top layer of the moat wall's bricks lay exposed to the sun. The old iron gate that blocked the sea from rushing in steamed as sunlight baked it for the first time in forever.

"Oh, crap," Nathan whispered.

He sprinted around the top of the fort, keeping an eye on the accelerating water in the moat beneath him. He rounded the last corner on Valadez's side. The mercenary looked up at him in a mix of anger and confusion.

"What the hell are you doing over here?"

Nathan pointed to a spot in the moat below. "Look there!"

The murky moat water rushed from both directions and disappeared at the moat's edge like it was running down a drain. The water shallowed and exposed a wide, dark opening.

"A sink hole?" Valadez said.

"I wish."

In an eruption of sand and water, a giant crab burst from the opening. It spread its front claws wide apart and hissed. The eyestalks turned in opposite directions, with one black, glossy eye each aimed at Valadez and Nathan.

The two scrambled down the stairs and took up position at an embrasure on the second tier. In a flash, Valadez snapped his rifle to his shoulder. He sent a fusillade of rounds down at the creature.

Bullets pinged and sang against the crab's shell. Ricochets smacked against the fort's masonry and sent puffs of dust and rock chips into the air. The crab recoiled and skittered sideways. It cleared the hole in the ground and a second crab appeared within it.

"Oh, hell no," Valadez said.

He retrieved a grenade from a cargo pocket, pulled the pin, and threw it down into the hole. Seconds later, it exploded with a stifled boom. A spray of muddy water vomited from the hole and splattered against the fort wall.

"Take that, you pieces of—"

The second crab burst out of the hole, fast and, from the shaking of its claws, furious.

"Way to piss it off," Nathan said.

The second crab sidestepped in the opposite direction from the first along the now empty moat. Claws clacked against stone. The rank stench of algae and rotting fish rose up from below.

Larsson bounded up behind them, his rifle at the ready. "What's the shooting about?"

"Crabs at the wall," Valadez said.

Larsson moved left, and then sent a hail of rounds down at one of the crabs. Valadez fired a burst at the other. Then he pulled his pistol from his holster and offered it to Nathan.

"Ever used one of these?" he said.

"I once shot a derringer at history camp," Nathan said.

"Wow, you're all sorts of useless." Valadez tossed him the gun. "Point and pull the trigger. A round's chambered."

Nathan caught the pistol and snapped off the safety.

"You got the common sense to only aim that at the crabs, I hope."

"Never been a fan of shellfish," Nathan said.

He peered out of the embrasure. No new crabs poked out of the hole. The two in the moat headed back to the center. Valadez and Larsson rained bursts of bullets down on each with little effect. Nathan lined the heavy pistol up on the leftmost crab and pulled the trigger. The gun barked and had way more kick than he'd expected based on the movies. He guessed the round hit the crab. He couldn't see how he could have missed. The crab didn't flinch.

"Grenades!" Larsson yelled.

He and Valadez both grabbed grenades from their pockets and pulled the pins. Larsson pointed left and they threw both at the leftmost crab. The grenades bounced down the fort wall and into the moat under the crab.

The grenades exploded almost as one. A flash and roar sounded under the crab. It hopped up, screamed, and flailed its front claws. Then it scampered right. It did not look wounded.

"We can't break the shell," Valadez said.

Valadez sent a burst of rounds down on the crab. Larsson unloaded on the one on the right. Nathan aimed for a crab's face and sent two bullets dead center. They had no effect.

The crab on the right climbed up on the bridge to the main gate. It reared back a claw and drove it into the thick oak doors. Wood splintered and iron hinges groaned. It drove the claw home twice more. But the doors held.

"The doors just totally paid for themselves," Nathan said.

"Solid doors and a high wall," Larsson said. "We can't kill them, but we're safe in here."

Then the crab on the left stretched out its front claws and began to climb up the side of Fort Jefferson.

CHAPTER 29

Larsson decided this was the perfect time to cut and run.

No weapon they had could penetrate the crab's armored shell. Valadez might hold them off for a while, but if they could climb the damn walls, eventually, they'd climb in. And then the big doors keeping the crabs out would turn into big doors holding the people inside with the crabs. And that would get ugly.

The crab continued its crawl up the wall. One eyestalk stared into an embrasure. It jabbed a claw halfway through another with an explosion of red brick dust. The crab rocked back and forth trying to free its stuck claw.

Larsson pointed his rifle out of the embrasure and unloaded twenty rounds point blank into the crab's shell. The crab shuddered under the impact, though no bullets penetrated. It lost its grip and slipped down the side of the fort. Its claw did not break free.

The air filled with the sharp report of cracking shell. The joints of the great claw split and separated. The crab fell and landed on its back in the muddy drained moat. Seven claws flailed in the air. Its dismembered eighth stayed wedged in the embrasure.

Larsson saw his opportunity. "We need ammo. Hold tight."

Before Valadez could reply, Larsson bolted down the steps and into the courtyard. He went to the pile of supplies but didn't touch one round of ammo. He grabbed the silver suitcase containing the lure controller and ran for the powder magazine. Once inside, he slammed the door, threw open the trapdoor, and scrambled down into the old CIA bunker. He didn't take out his flashlight. He wouldn't be in the dark long enough to need one.

Once inside, he stopped in front of the air vent. He untied a shoelace and tied one end to the metal briefcase's handle. Then Larsson climbed into the vent head-first and arms up. His gut wedged tight between the sides. With a back and forth shimmy like a rotund snake, he worked his way down the air vent. When his feet disappeared inside, his shoelace dragged the controller along behind him.

He worked his way to where the vent turned straight up and bright daylight illuminated the space. With great effort, he forced himself through the constricting turn and swore he'd lose ten pounds when this was over.

He crawled up and out of the shaft. It seemed like he'd stepped into a junkyard. He peered over the top of the trash. He had a clear line of sight of the whole area, and an open path to the beach. The Zodiac sat on the sand, loaded with most of the lures. The incoming tide had lifted the stern free.

At the fort, the crab that had lost its claw still lay on its back, but two others skittered back and forth along the moat. A hand grenade sailed out of one embrasure. It landed beside one crab and exploded with zero effect. A pistol barked from another embrasure. Its rounds just ricocheted off the crab's shell.

The two in the fort would be too busy to notice his departure until it was too late. The crabs had opted to attack through tunnels into the moat, which he hoped meant they'd left the beach unoccupied. His path to vengeance was clear and calling to him.

"No time like the present," Larsson said to himself.

He vaulted over an empty metal drum and sprinted for the beach with the controller in his hand.

CHAPTER 30

Nathan knew a losing battle when he saw one.

He'd read enough accounts of them, from Brandywine Creek to Gettysburg to the Argonne Forest. Soldiers on the losing side got to a point where the outcome, though perhaps still distant, now manifested as inevitable. This fight between three men and giant crabs had reached that point.

Another crab had just crawled out of the hole, as if it had been in the bullpen waiting to replace the one now trapped on its back.

He leaned out the embrasure and fired several bullets at the crab in the moat, hoping to find some tiny chink in its impenetrable armor. The crab continued to search the outer wall for a good grip to start its climb. Three men weren't going to hold those things off.

In the distance, he caught sight of Larsson running from the north coaling station ruins to the beach, carrying a silver briefcase. He did a double take. *Wasn't Larsson down below getting ammo?* He glanced over his shoulder and saw an empty parade ground.

"Check the beach!" he shouted at Valadez.

Valadez ripped a half dozen rounds at the closest crab and then looked out across the key. His face reddened. "That deserting son of a bitch."

Larsson reached the Zodiac and threw the silver case in the back. He grabbed the rifle from near Wilson's corpse. Nathan held out hope that a giant crab would rise from the sea and tear the man in half. It didn't happen. Larsson jumped in and started the engine. He backed the nose of the inflatable off the beach.

Nathan wouldn't miss Larsson, but his departure left them a man short and still low on ammunition. And the crabs kept coming.

He emptied the rest of his clip into the face of the crab in the moat. It flinched, found footing, and started to climb.

He dropped the clip from the pistol and saw that it was empty.

"Need one of these?" Gianna said from behind him.

Nathan turned and she held out two clips. Four new ammunition cans sat at her feet. He was torn between joy over the reload and fear over her exposure. He grabbed the clips.

"How the hell did you get here?" Valadez said. "You drowned in the trawler."

He leveled his rifle at Gianna. Nathan grabbed the barrel and pushed it skyward.

"How about we focus on the crabs?" Nathan said. He turned to Gianna. "We need more grenades."

She nodded and headed back down the steps. Nathan kicked a can of rifle ammunition over to Valadez. With fury in his eyes, Valadez watched Gianna leave.

"It'll take all of us to get out of this alive," Nathan said.

"It might take more than that," Valadez replied.

He pulled a grenade from his pocket and yanked the pin. He leaned out the embrasure and with an underhand lob tossed the grenade between the climbing crab to the left and the fortress wall. The blast propelled the crab off the brick in a cloud of red clay dust. It dropped into the moat and immediately righted itself and threw itself back into the attack. Valadez turned to Nathan and smiled.

"Now that felt good," he said.

Suddenly, behind him, a claw burst through the embrasure. It snapped closed around his waist. He screamed as the claw pulled him back out. His head slammed against the bricks and he went limp.

Gianna reappeared with two cans of grenades. She dropped them and screamed at the sight of Valadez in the crab's claw outside the wall.

Nathan knew they were doomed. There was no way he and Gianna could hold off these crabs. He wondered how the soldiers in the fort ever had. The grenades had enough kick to knock the crabs off the wall, but not enough to kill them.

The crab shoved Valadez's body into its mouth. Then it rammed its blood-soaked claw back through the embrasure. It missed Nathan by inches.

Then he had an idea.

"Bring those grenades," he said to Gianna.

Nathan ran up the stairs to the terreplein. Gianna followed with the grenade cans. He went to the big restored Rodman gun. A stack of cannon balls stood behind it. He picked up one ball. It had to weigh fifty pounds. His back complained, but all that weight was just what he'd hoped for.

Eyestalks peered over the edge in front of the cannon. Then the crab raised itself up over the terreplein's edge, exposing the white underside of its shell.

"Pull the pins and drop two grenades down the barrel," Nathan said. "Now!"

Gianna grabbed two grenades and pulled the pins. The handles sailed off into space. She dropped them down the barrel and turned away with her ears covered. Nathan rolled the cannonball down the barrel and dove flat on the ground. The ball clunked against the grenades. He covered his ears.

The grenades boomed. The cannonball rocketed out of the barrel. The gun rocked backward with the recoil. Paint around the wheels shattered into black snowflakes.

The cannonball slammed the crab in the underbelly. It tore through the shell in an explosion of pink meat and clear liquid. The impact drove the creature off the wall, and it tumbled down into the moat.

Gianna looked up and out across the empty horizon. She raised a fist in victory. "Yes!"

To the left, the second crab crawled up onto the terreplein. Its rear legs sent a cascade of loose bricks down into the moat as it crawled onto the fort. The twin eyestalks turned and stopped, fixing on Gianna and Nathan.

"Pivot the cannon!" Nathan jumped up and pushed the cannon right along the race. Rust ground around the cannon's carriage. Gianna pitched in and it lurched to a stop facing the advancing crab.

Gianna needed no orders. She dropped two more sputtering grenades into the barrel. Nathan grabbed another ball. The iron slipped against his sweat-soaked palms. He dropped the ball in front of the cannon.

The crab hissed, spread its claws, and rushed the cannon.

Nathan scooped the cannonball up and heaved it down the barrel. He dropped to the ground. Before the ball could hit the barrel's bottom, the grenades exploded.

The cannonball blasted over him so closely that its wake rippled his shirt. The ball struck the crab just below the eyes and caved in what passed as its face. One claw took a clumsy swipe at the cannon and missed. The crab staggered sideways and stumbled off into the parade ground below. It hit the grass with a sound like a breaking eggshell. It lay on its back and did not move.

Nathan crawled over to the edge and looked out. From within the hole in the moat, another crab moved.

"Hell, no," Nathan said.

He had to refill the moat, and there was only one way to do that. Open the iron gate in the moat wall. The one that had long ago rusted permanently shut.

He pulled a hand grenade from the box and practically tumbled down the steps to the ground level. He ran for the hole in the south bastion, slipped through, and dashed across the silt bridge to the moat wall.

He sprinted down the moat wall toward the gate. With yards to go, his foot hit a loose brick. The brick slid. He skated sideways. The grenade went sailing into space, and he tumbled into the empty moat.

Nathan splatted face first in a layer of fetid ooze. He rose and spit something rank from his lips. The grenade lay embedded a few feet away. His feet slipped as he fought for grip in the muck. He scrambled to the grenade and dug it from the mud. With a lurch, he slogged to the iron gate. Standing on the moat bottom, it was over his head.

"Son of a…"

His plan was to be watching the moat when it refilled. Instead, he'd be swimming in it. If he could.

He pulled the pin on the grenade, jumped, and wedged it in the gate's corner. He landed in the mud and fell back on his butt.

The grenade exploded. Shards of iron sang as they sailed past his head. Seawater blasted through the opening like it came from a firehose. The pressure swept away crumbling mortar and then bricks around the opening washed away. The incoming sea swelled to a torrent and knocked Nathan flat on his back. The water spun him against the slick, algae-coated walls and then drove him down along the moat. His head submerged.

In the cloudy, rushing water, he could not tell up from down, heard nothing but the pounding of water against stone, and felt nothing but the scrape of his tumbling body across the moat wall. And somewhere up ahead, all this water funneled into a hole filled with giant crabs.

Something caught the collar of his shirt. He stopped moving but the rushing water threatened to pull him out of his clothes. He reached up to grab this lifeline and felt an arm. It pulled and he broke the surface.

Gianna held him with one hand and had the other clamped to the bridge to the main gate. Nathan coughed out a mouthful of saltwater. He grabbed a crumbled edge of the moat and together they pulled him out.

The churning moat water forced a half-exposed crab back down into the hole in the moat. Then the force eroded the sides and the hole collapsed. The moat refilled to sea level and the water calmed.

They made their way back along the edge of the fort and through the hole in the south bastion. Inside, they collapsed in the sun on the parade ground. The dead crab lay a dozen yards away.

Nathan could barely believe that he was still alive.

"Are you okay?" Gianna said.

"I think so. You?"

She pattered herself down and looked incredulous. "Somehow, yes."

Nathan looked across the fort and up at the Rodman gun they'd used to kill the crabs. "Nineteenth-century tech and it still worked. They don't make 'em like that anymore."

"I think we broke it," Gianna said.

She was right. The cannon would never fire again. Missing patches of restoration paint revealed new, deep cracks in the cast iron. The metal band along the rear had separated from the barrel.

"It gave its life so others could live," Nathan said. "After a century and a half of waiting."

He rose and climbed to an embrasure overlooking the east beach. The moat remained crab-free. Out past the shore, Larsson and the Zodiac filled with lures were clearing the edge of the key.

"We won the battle, but lost the war," he said. "Larsson is heading out to sea with the lures. What we just survived is about to happen all across south Florida."

CHAPTER 31

When he was young, swimming underwater had been Marc Metcalf's peaceful place.

From his rookie dive decades ago, the sense of pressure and isolation that gave many the creeps about being below the surface imbued him with serenity. All noise was muted, all motions fluid, and being weightless instilled wonder. Was he subconsciously returning to the womb, as some had told him? He preferred to not entertain that explanation.

But now, diving was a reminder that he wasn't that young man anymore. The sense of relief at taking the weight off his hips and knees when he began to float. The extra concentration it took to breathe through lungs that didn't have the capacity of youth. The ocean's cold that now penetrated deeper than when he'd had the protection of more fat and muscle. The fear that today would be the day the elements took an extra toll on his weakened heart.

He tugged the cable after him as he swam down from his cabin cruiser. He focused on the rhythm of his breathing to quell the fear about what lay ahead. He had nowhere near the confidence he'd shown Kathy that they were going to pull this off.

The sea grew darker and he clicked on the lights on his wrists. Ahead loomed the outline of PT 904 on the sea floor. Or at least half of it. He'd found the bow section. When the crab tore the ship in half, he guessed the current had swept this section away from the heavier, faster sinking stern, which likely lay elsewhere alongside the remains of PT 906.

The boat seemed more reef than ship after so many years underwater. Barnacles and coral nobs coated the hull. Strands of seaweed swayed in the current as if waving a greeting to PT 904's only remaining crewmember. She lay on her port side, buried several feet deep in the sand, but the object of Marc's quest appeared unharmed. A twenty-foot-long starboard torpedo tube. The covers were still in place, so the torpedo had to still be inside, right where he'd loaded it a lifetime ago.

He swam down and floated beside the tube. He drew his knife and scraped the boat's deck with the blade, chipping away the encrustation to reveal the painted wood beneath. Marc rolled off his glove and laid his fingertips against the ship.

So long ago, my girl, he thought.

He and the others had been kids playing spies on a big power boat. Immortal and unbreakable. Now his body constantly reminded him that he was neither, and the wreckage reminded him that of the crew only he remained. In the years since then, he'd added nothing of consequence to the world, nothing worthy of the memories of the men who died here while he was condemned to live.

I'm gonna fix that now.

He pulled his glove back on. Using the knife hilt, he hammered at the clamps that held the torpedo cover in place. He snapped one, then the other. He cut away the canvas covers at the ends of the tube and pulled it open.

Protected from the open sea and any larger organisms, the torpedo looked almost good as new. A light film of bright green algae covered the surface, but the torpedo was free of any larger marine life. To the rear, the twin screw propellers and the directional fins around them shined.

He wrapped the canvas straps around the torpedo, then kicked free the clamps that held it in place. He scraped his knife against the cable to send the pull signal back to Kathy topside.

The cable tightened. Marc guided the torpedo up from the mounts and then pushed it clear of the wreck. The cable continued to retract and the torpedo began its slow ascent to the daylight it hadn't seen in five decades.

Marc turned to look at the wreck below him. Tommy and Bud had died right there, yanked out of those forward gun positions. Matty had been chopped in two on that bow. The sea and all within it had long ago claimed their flesh and bones. But maybe there would be something personal from each he could gather, something to return to their families to remind them of the men's sacrifice.

He nosed down and swam to the stern of the wreck. The cabin was black as a cavern in front of him. Sea life had taken residence all along the bulkheads and anemones and clownfish did little dances along the rim. He swam in a few feet and pointed the wrist lights into the forward berth.

They lit the menacing snout of a full-grown bull shark.

CHAPTER 32

The shark's mouth opened to reveal rows of razor-sharp teeth.

Marc's heart jumped to triple-speed. Bull sharks were the worst combination of aggressive and unpredictable. He yelped an explosion of bubbles past his regulator and backpedaled away.

He couldn't move fast enough. The shark lunged from the darkness. Marc spun left and the shark's stout body scraped across his chest as it rushed by. Its rough hide shredded his aging wetsuit and dug into Marc's skin beneath. Its tail smacked him on the sidestroke and spun him in a circle.

The shark rocketed into the sea and turned for another attack. Marc backed away and too late realized he'd swum back into the wreck. He looked out through the open hull like Jonah from the mouth of the whale. The shark headed straight for him.

Marc realized his knife was useless. He frantically checked the wreck for a weapon. The shark closed to yards away.

Marc spied an old combat helmet half-buried in the sand. He yanked it out and faced the shark.

At mere feet away, the shark's jaws snapped open. Marc whipped the coral-encrusted helmet up and shoved it straight ahead. The shark's jaws clamped down on the steel. The furious fish snapped its head back and forth to dislodge the helmet. Marc let it go but a row of teeth ripped across his hand like a chainsaw blade and severed his ring and pinky fingers. Pain blasted up his arm and lanced his skull.

The shark backed off, jerking left and right to try to dislodge the crushed helmet wedged in its jaws.

Red wisps of blood leaked from the finger stubs on Marc's right hand. All he could imagine was the blood drawing more sharks. He gripped his wounds with his left hand to stem the bleeding. Then he beat the sea with his swim fins and headed for the surface.

Below him, the bull shark circled the wreck doing a series of frustrated snaps of its head, each unable to spit out the helmet.

With an adrenaline-fueled surge of energy, Marc swam for his life. His heart slammed in his chest and sharp needles of pain accompanied each beat. He caught up with the rising torpedo and hooked his arm through one of the cargo straps. The strengthening stabs to his heart and the exhaustion of receding panic took its toll. He collapsed and let the rising torpedo bring him the rest of the way home.

***

Kathy slowed the winch as the torpedo came close enough for her to make out the details. It was much larger than she'd expected. Marc clung to one of the straps, and he wasn't moving.

She bumped the winch speed back up. The torpedo broke the surface with Marc almost draped across it. He spit his regulator from his mouth and flashed her a look of pained relief through his facemask. Deep red blood ran from his right hand and down the torpedo's mossy green side.

She stopped the winch and swung the torpedo closer to the side of the boat. Marc crawled across it to the ladder at the rear. He climbed on board using only one hand. His bleeding right was missing two fingers. His wetsuit top had been shredded and blood seeped from deep scratches along his chest.

Kathy gasped. "What happened?"

"Shark." Marc wheezed out a long breath. "I'm okay."

Marc's face was bone-white and the last thing he seemed was okay. She pulled him up and into the cockpit. As soon as she unstrapped the scuba tank from his back, he collapsed to the deck, his back against the stern.

"There's a first-aid kit in the forward cabin," he said through clenched teeth.

Kathy scrambled to find the kit. When she returned, the old man had shed the top half of his wetsuit and both gloves. His left hand clamped his right, but blood still dripped onto the deck. The chest wound was superficial. But the missing fingers gave her pause. She knelt beside him.

"Let me check that out," she whispered.

He extended his right hand. The two fingers had been severed at the second joint. She disinfected the wound with alcohol and bound the fingers with a roll of gauze. By the time she finished, just two fingers and a thumb stuck out of a tight, white ball. The good news was that the white wasn't turning red. She'd at least slowed the bleeding from a rush to a seep, and she'd take that small victory.

Marc rooted in the kit with his good hand and retrieved an unmarked prescription bottle. He popped the top and downed two pills. He caught Kathy staring at him.

"Painkillers," he said. "You're gonna be out alone on the sea, you gotta be prepared for emergencies."

"I think this qualifies."

"Trust me that I need 'em."

Kathy looked over the side at the torpedo. "Is it in good shape?"

"Good as the last day I saw it. I need to pull it open and double-check some things." With his good hand, he pulled himself up into a seat.

"Whoa!" Kathy said. "You need to go below and lay down."

"No time for that nonsense." The color had begun to return to his face. "I got a torpedo to work on. You need to get us to Crab Central. Head south-southeast until we round Bush Key. Then we'll use that map of yours to plot the last leg of the trip."

Marc pulled a screwdriver from a locker in the cockpit. He winched the torpedo up even with the boat's transom, then leaned over and began to scrape the drying algae from the body. He winced with every stroke.

"Let me give you a hand," Kathy offered.

"Dammit, no! I'll do this. You weigh anchor and get the damn boat where we need to go. Or I'll just do everything and you can go below."

She hadn't seen even a flicker of anger in Marc. Maybe being mutilated by the shark had given him more of a brush with mortality than he wanted to admit, or visiting the wreck reminded him about the friends he'd lost on PT 904. He needed a solo win working on the torpedo to get his confidence back.

She walked to the bow and began to reel in the anchor line. She looked over her shoulder, through the glazed windscreen, at Marc in the stern. He leaned over the torpedo, loosening an access panel with the screwdriver.

The only things that stood between the world and an onslaught of giant crabs were her, a wounded old man, an obsolete torpedo, and a boat that was already old when the Beach Boys had hit songs.

Those odds weren't good.

***

Marc's hand shook as he loosened the screw on the access panel. He paused and took a deep breath. His right hand felt like it was on fire. It would have been nice if the pills he'd taken *had* been painkillers. But it was better that they had been his nitroglycerin. Given a choice between being alive with a beating heart and being in pain with severed fingers, alive was much better.

But he feared that soon he wouldn't even have that. He'd had years of what he'd called heart episodes. What had happened underwater had been more than an episode. The water pressure, the panic, the exertion. A trifecta of triggers, all at once. He could feel the damage, the weakened, irregular pulsing in his chest.

Now he raced two clocks, the clock ticking up to a mass escape of crabs, and his personal clock that was ticking down. He had to coax the second clock to keep ticking a little longer.

The screwdriver tip slipped out of the screw head. The tool flew from his hand. He slapped it tight against the torpedo with his bad hand just before it fell into the sea. Pain set his arm ablaze. He clenched his teeth against a scream.

Dread tightened in his gut. He may have found the location of the crabs' den too late.

CHAPTER 33

An hour later, Kathy left the wheel to check on Marc's progress, physically as well as on the torpedo. He looked better, but he still winced every time his injured hand touched something.

"The torpedo still works?" she asked.

Marc pressed the screwdriver against two exposed wires inside one of the access panels. The torpedo's twin propellers kicked into a furious spin.

"The main battery stayed watertight. I got it recharged. It won't have the range to knock out Russian subs, but it'll get far enough to keep us out of the blast range. But the 26-volt system is shot to hell, so rigging up any steering is out of the question, even if I had a controller."

"So how do we get the thing to hit the crab den?"

Marc gave her a wink. "We do it the old fashioned way. Point and shoot. We line up the boat and send the fish a-swimming."

"That'll work?"

"We won two world wars doing it that way."

"And the warhead?"

"I checked. Strictly conventional, designed to crush a sub from concussion. Perfect to collapse underground tunnels and seal them crabs back inside. We're gonna be perfectly safe."

Kathy didn't feel even imperfectly safe. Messing with a salvaged torpedo carrying a fifty-year-old bomb in the nose seemed like courting disaster.

Kathy returned to the wheel. Fort Jefferson passed by the port side, a mile or two away. Kathy tried the radio, but as it had been the whole trip, all she heard was static and squeal. Larsson's jammer could work as far away as Key West for all she knew.

A brass telescope stuck out from a pouch by the steering wheel. Of course the eccentric old man would have an unconventional telescope instead of conventional binoculars. With her hip against the wheel, she trained the telescope on the fort and twisted the building into focus.

The heavy main doors were closed, but they sported some big gashes. A dead crab lay upside down, half out of the moat. There might have been two, it was hard to tell. Chunks of missing brick left bright red gouges in the walls, like fresh, painful wounds. The battle the fort had been built to withstand had finally come and gone, and the fort had survived. Her fear was about what happened to Nathan inside. Larsson's pseudo-soldiers might be able to handle themselves in a fight against the crabs. The little historian? She wasn't so sure.

She lowered the telescope and checked the rear of the cockpit. The old man leaned across the transom performing a one-handed wiring job on the torpedo. Drops of his blood had spotted the deck. She wondered how she'd ever thought this plan could work.

"Marc! Chart check time. We're due south of the fort."

Marc looked up at her and squinted against the sun. Then he looked toward the fort. His eyes went wide and his jaw dropped.

"What the hell are you doing! Turn to starboard!"

Kathy looked at the placid water all around them. A few ripples danced on the surface just ahead. "What's wrong?"

Marc sprang to his feet and rushed to the wheel. He brushed Kathy aside and spun the wheel to the right.

The boat heeled starboard and the props growled at the change in direction. Then from below came the crash and crack of snapping wood. The boat shuddered as a reef scraped hard against the hull.

"Dammit to hell," Marc shouted. "Don't you know there's a reef out here?"

He dropped the engines to idle and scrambled down into the cabin. He pulled an access panel up from the floor. Water rushed in the bilge underneath.

"Pumps! On the console, turn on the pumps!"

Kathy scanned the controls. Two switches labeled BIL PUMP STAR and BIL PUMP PORT were under the water temperature gauge. She flicked both on.

Electric motors hummed to life under the deck. Air and water coughed out of an exhaust port on the boat's side. A moment later, Marc came back topside.

"They're barely keeping up, especially with the weight of the torpedo across the stern. Were you trying to sink us?"

"How was I supposed to know there's a reef out here? We're far from the key."

"It's your damn park, your protected ocean. Besides, you couldn't read the water and see it was shallow ahead?"

She remembered the ripples in the water just before the crash. "Maybe. I'm no sailor. I don't understand half the things going on out here."

Marc was about to deliver another admonishment but cut himself short. He exhaled hard and some of the fury drained from his face. A few brighter blood spots stippled the drying scabs on his chest.

"Well, you're right there. I ain't sailed with a crew in fifty years, and never had one that wasn't rated at sea. I shoulda warned you about the reef. I was all caught up in wiring the fish."

He rolled the engines back to full speed and turned the boat due east. "Okay, let's see your map now."

Kathy took out the map she'd stolen from the old CIA base and spread it out on the little chart table beside the ship's wheel. She reached over and held the wheel while Marc used a ruler, a pencil and the compass to find the boat's position relative to the fort and the ripples of the retreating shoal. He marked that spot and drew a line from it to the location of the crabs' den.

"Zero-four-seven degrees," he said. "That's our course, correcting for the currents." He turned the wheel and rolled the boat out on a forty-seven-degree compass heading.

Kathy glanced down into the cabin. Water bubbled up from the bilge and onto the lower deck. "Marc, the pumps aren't keeping up."

Marc peered over from the wheel. "Damn, it's the speed, the extra pressure against the hull. We're gonna need to slow down."

"We don't have time." Kathy jumped down into the cabin. Underway, the cabin stank of oil and unburned gasoline. She pulled a big plastic bowl from the tiny kitchen area. She dipped it into the bilge. When it filled with water, she dumped it into the cockpit. The water ran back to the stern and drained out a hole through the transom.

"Now that might be the ticket," Marc said. "That chore'll keep you busy."

"As long as it keeps us afloat, and you keep us on course."

"Aye, aye. Zero-four-seven it is."

Below deck, the thrum of the engine was much louder than in the cockpit. With little ventilation, the petroleum stink and manifold heat had nowhere to go, and the cabin quickly turned oppressive. Kathy began scooping and sloshing seawater from the cabin floor to the cockpit, like a character from some old-time cartoon.

She remembered that the boat always sank in those stories.

CHAPTER 34

The Zodiac pounded through the waves north of Garden Key. For the first time in months, Larsson felt, dare he say it, happy.

So much had gone so wrong. The crabs' premature escape. The rush to get his team assembled. The loss of the trawler. The crashed helicopter. That bitch of a park ranger discovering the hidden room. But despite it all, here he was, with the lures, heading out to drop them as planned, and start the crabs on a path of chaotic destruction across Florida.

Had there been losses executing his plan? Sure, but weren't eggs broken to make an omelet? Anything this risky carried a downside potential. But everyone he'd hired or recruited should have weighed the odds when they started, the potential consequences if things moved a little off-center. Their deaths could not have surprised them, and the plan's success would make the sacrifices all worthwhile.

The GPS in the Zodiac blinked and indicated he'd arrived at the first waypoint. Time to drop Lure #1. He throttled back the engine to idle. From the stern, he picked the top lure off the stack. With a flick of a switch on the side, he powered up the sonic transmitter. The indicator light flashed yellow, then green. Ready to rock.

He went to the controller and turned on the switch for that lure. The light beside the switch turned yellow, then red.

Larsson ground his teeth. He didn't know exactly how this whole system worked, but he sure as hell knew that it didn't work like this. Step one was two green lights. Without that, there was no step two.

He cycled the switches on both units. The lure turned green again, the controller did not. He cursed and tossed the lure aside. He tried a second lure, then the rest. Same results every time. Active lures, no contact with the controller.

He cursed and pounded the side of the inflatable with his fists. "No, no, no! Not after everything that happened, not after getting so close."

The controller, that had to be it. It had to have been damaged in the crash. Why the hell hadn't he taken both controllers? No point in having a backup if you didn't have the backup with you, was there?

He checked his watch. There was still enough daylight to get back, get the controller, and keep the plan rolling forward. By now, everyone who remained behind would have been reduced to crab food, and the crabs would have moved on to new prey. He hoped. He wouldn't need much time anyway. In, grab the controller, and out.

He rolled the engine up to full power, turned the Zodiac around, and set a course for Garden Key.

***

The dead crab on the parade ground reeked. The cannonball had torn a hole through it and the stink of crab and seawater seemed to fill the fort's interior. Flies buzzed in the air.

Nathan's personal turn in the moat muck only add to the aroma. He wrinkled his nose in disgust. "I think this experience has taken crab off my menu forever."

He joined Gianna at the stack of supplies salvaged from the downed helicopter. They sorted through the remaining crates to see what ammunition was available to fend off the next attack. There wasn't much.

"There's going to be panic and chaos when those crabs hit a populated area," Nathan said.

"Nothing to worry about. While the three of you were beating back the first crab attack, I saw my chance, snuck out, and reset the controllers to the wrong addresses. They won't turn anything on, and Larsson doesn't know enough about how they work to be able to reprogram them."

"I'm going to go out on a limb and guess that that's going to really piss him off."

Gianna smiled. "I was hoping it would."

Nathan's face fell. "But then he'll be coming right back here. And even two-on-one, I don't like our odds against him in a firefight."

"And we could face more crabs before that happens."

Nathan thought a moment. "There are still some lures on the beach. Looks like they were left here because they were damaged. Think you can make one that works?"

"I can try. And I can reset the backup controller here to the right arming address. Why would we want to lure the crabs back here?"

"We wouldn't. The Park Service skiff is hidden under the dock. We can load the lure and take it out to deeper water. We turn it on and at least we could direct the crabs somewhere away from civilization long enough to set the rest of the world to work killing them."

"I think that I like that plan."

"At a minimum, it beats waiting here to be killed by Larsson or a giant crab. Let's make it happen."

***

Larsson closed on Garden Key. Through binoculars, the fort looked deserted and far worse for the wear of the giant crab attack. Two crab corpses lay beside the moat. Looked like Valadez had gotten two before the rest got him. Good for Valadez.

From this angle, he couldn't really see the east beach, but he could see that the island was crab-free. That was good. His plan for a touch-and-go to grab the controller would work just fine.

He looked down to check the radar and noticed a blip for a boat off the key's southern coast. It was heading northeast, dead on the compass heading for the crab's underwater den.

That couldn't be a coincidence. The only boat out here is heading straight for Crab City? Maybe the History Ranger had survived, defeated the radio jamming, and called in help. Then again, he'd never come across Kathy's body, so maybe she had swum for help. More likely than either scenario, it was some random pleasure boater. But at this point, he wasn't taking any chances.

First step, make certain his supply of crabs would be uninterrupted. Second step, return to the key for the lure's controller.

He turned the boat southeast, away from the fort, and prepared to intercept whoever it was trying to throw one last monkey wrench into his plan.

CHAPTER 35

"Okay, you're gonna need to give that a rest for a bit," Marc said.

Kathy was ready to. Her back and arms burned from the constant stoop-and-slosh bailing of the flooding cabin. The engine fumes made her dizzy, and the closed space made her nauseous. But she was barely keeping ahead of the rising water.

"I can't," she said.

"Ain't no choice in it. We gotta get the torpedo in position."

Kathy set the plastic bowl on the deck and climbed up into the fresh air and sunlight. She really wished she had her hat.

"Now you gotta swing the winch around so the torpedo is nose-first along the starboard side. Once we find the crabs' den, I'll circle back around, line the boat up for the shot, and let the fish do the rest."

It seemed like there had to be more to firing torpedoes than that, but she had to trust that Marc knew what he was doing. He had so far.

She went back to the rear, steadied the torpedo with one hand, and tried to swing the winch around with the other. It didn't budge.

She gripped the winch with both hands, wedged her feet against the cockpit, and pulled. Still nothing.

"When was the last time you moved this thing?" she asked Marc.

"I move it all the time...or I used to...well, now that I think of it...might have been a while."

She gripped the winch again, flexed her knees to put her legs into the effort, and pulled. The winch broke free and swung around. She tried to stop it, but the momentum of the heavy torpedo was too great. It slammed sideways against the hull of the boat with a loud boom.

"What are you doing back there?"

Kathy looked over the side. Marc had hung three white, round dock bumpers along the side of the boat. Now the one furthest back looked like a deflated balloon.

"It's okay. The bumpers saved us. When did you put them out there?"

"While you were bailing. Let me fill you in on Rule #1 from torpedoman school. Never sink your boat with your own torpedo."

"I'll keep that in mind." Kathy tied the winch in place with the line from the burst dock bumper. She wasn't going to take the chance that it might decide to move easier on its own than it had with her assistance.

When she'd finished, she checked over the side and looked down into the water, so clear that she could see over twenty feet down, though through the churn of the boat's wake everything shimmered. On the sandy bottom, something moved.

She looked closer. It was a giant crab, moving in the opposite direction. Once she recognized the one, it was as if her eyes had been opened. Suddenly, she could see a half dozen spread out across the sea floor.

"Marc, we have a problem down there."

"Not as big as the one I'm seeing up here."

She doubted that. She looked up, and she was wrong. A grey Zodiac bore down on them. She grabbed the telescope and trained it on the boat. Larsson's angry face was unmistakable, as was the rifle slung across his shoulder. The faster Zodiac was closing on the *Solitude*.

"Do you have any guns aboard?" Kathy asked.

"Never carry one. We got a torpedo, though."

"That's not going to help. That's Larsson. He's not going to be happy about us trying to screw up his plan."

"You don't get back to bailing, we'll sink before he catches us."

Kathy looked down into the cabin. The plastic bowl floated on water six inches deep.

"Dammit!" She jumped down and landed on the lower deck with a splash. She snatched the bowl from the water and began bailing furiously.

All their effort and sacrifice was about to be for nothing.

CHAPTER 36

"There you go, good as new."

Gianna lifted up a finished lure from the parts she'd scavenged from two. She flipped a switch on the side and a green light illuminated. She flashed a proud smile.

"You didn't just send an all-crabs-on-deck call did you?" Nathan said.

"No, that only happens when I activate it from the controller. I reset this lure to a unique address and set the controller to that same address. We drop it somewhere deep, scoot away, and turn it on from a distance. Crabs should come running."

"From how far away?"

"Miles. Sound really travels in water."

"Something else I learned today. I might turn into the Science Ranger Geek in spite of myself."

"I don't get that."

"Inside joke between me and Larsson. Ready to go play Pied Piper to crabs?"

"Let's use my skills for good instead of evil."

Nathan scooped up the controller briefcase and a rifle, and headed to where the skiff was nosed up on the sand. He'd brought it around to the east beach while Gianna worked on the lure. He sat in the skiff's stern and started the motor. Gianna tossed the lure in the bow, pushed the boat into the water, and climbed in.

Nathan gunned the engine and headed them east away from the fort.

"So is being a park ranger always this exciting?" Gianna said.

"This? This is a slow day. I feel guilty even getting a paycheck if this is all I have to do."

"Do you think anyone will believe this latest chapter in the history of Fort Jefferson when you tell it?"

"I'm not sure that I believe it, and I'm living it. What about you? Anyone going to believe you when you go back to Silenius Imports and tell them you were kidnapped and then fought off giant crabs?"

"Given all the secret projects they work on, I think they might believe me. But this brush with black operations has convinced me to find a safer line of work."

"Like cleaning up nuclear waste spills aboard space stations about to crash to Earth?"

"Yes, safer like that."

Gianna looked over the side of the boat and gasped. She shuffled back to the middle. "We might not need the lure to find crabs."

Nathan glanced over the stern. The clear, shallow water was about fifteen feet deep. A giant crab crawled by underneath them. Another followed right behind it.

"We got off the beach in time," Nathan said. "And those crabs prove more are coming. We need to act fast to draw them out into deeper water."

Far off to port, a boat appeared, low to the water, heading southeast at a faster rate than the skiff. Nathan put the binoculars to his eyes. His heart sank. It looked like the Zodiac Larsson had escaped in.

"Is that a boat over there?" Gianna said. "Help is on the way?"

"If by 'help' you mean 'catastrophic hindrance' then, yeah, it's on the way."

He handed her the binoculars. She trained them on the boat and cursed. "That's Larsson in that Zodiac. I can see the stack of red and white lures in the back."

"But the fort is behind us and there's just open water ahead. Where's he going in such a hurry?"

Gianna turned around and trained the binoculars ahead. "Wait. There's a boat out there as well. A power boat, like an old cabin cruiser. Looks like a big winch coming up from the stern."

"Whoa, that's Metcalf's boat. Kathy's on board. If she's heading out to sea, she's got a plan to stop this disaster. And if Larsson is racing to intercept, he's worried she might succeed."

"She and this Metcalf can hold Larsson off?"

"Metcalf's probably an octogenarian, and Kathy's unarmed. I paint their situation as bleak. We're fast enough to catch up with Metcalf's boat, but the Zodiac will get there long before we do."

Too far away to help, but close enough to see Kathy die. After all he'd been through, it couldn't end like that.

CHAPTER 37

"Wait!" Gianna said. "I have an idea."

She put the controller briefcase on her lap and popped it open. She raised a small panel door in the lower corner and reset some pin switches. The panel dropped back down with a click and the buttons of the controller lit up.

"Are you going to set off our lure?"

"Nah." She pointed the briefcase toward the speeding Zodiac. "I'll reset the addresses to the other lures. I'm going to set off his."

***

Larsson saw a second, smaller blip appear on his radar to the southwest. He cast a quick glance in that direction, but nothing caught his eye. He returned his focus to the cabin cruiser dead ahead. He trained his binoculars on the boat's cockpit. There was no mistaking it. That bitch park ranger had somehow gotten on board the boat.

Well, that was just going to make this even more fun. Finally, everything was coming up Larsson.

Something buzzed behind him. He turned to see one of the lures at the bottom of the pile vibrating. Its solid green light now flashed. He looked at his controller. The lights were still red.

"How the hell...?"

He gave the lure a kick. It kept humming.

"First I couldn't turn one on, now I can't turn one off. Of all the malfunctioning crap..."

He realized he needed to get the thing off his boat before crabs began to congregate at the signal. He stepped away from the wheel and yanked the lure out from the bottom of the pile. He heaved it as far away from the boat as possible. It sailed through the air, end over end.

Just before it hit the water, a huge claw broke the surface and snapped it in half.

A second, and then a third lure began to buzz and flash at his feet. His heart leaped into his throat. He'd be crab food before he got all of them overboard.

He turned back to the controls and jammed the throttle against the forward stop, though the engine was already wide open. He glanced over the starboard side. A crab scrambled along the sea floor. Off to port, another scurried through the sand.

The rest of the lures went active. The pile sounded like a hive of furious wasps.

The crabs couldn't swim. At least he was pretty sure, based on the CIA documents, that they couldn't swim. He needed to get to deeper water. He just didn't know where that was. All the waters around the Keys seemed to randomly get shallow.

He clicked on the depth finder. The red number read fifteen feet. He'd need way more than that. Other crabs joined the chase after the Zodiac.

The depth finder flashed red. The number changed to ten, then nine, then eight.

"Oh, hell." Larsson spun the wheel.

Larsson's turn was too late. A crab burst up out of the sea straight ahead. It screamed a hiss like escaping steam. One claw swept across the sea and hit the Zodiac square on the side. The little boat went airborne and launched Larsson into the water. He went under.

Underwater, he couldn't hear the lures, but he could feel them. With so many so close, the water vibrated all around him.

The weight of the rifle across his back dragged him down. He struggled to pull it over his head. His feet touched sand and he finally freed himself. He reached to swim for the surface, his lungs begging for air.

A crab stared him down from a foot away. Panic froze him in place.

Claws slashed through the sea. Blue water turned blood red, and then everything went dark.

***

From the skiff, it looked like the Zodiac disappeared in an explosion of white water and giant claws. Crabs crawled all over the wreckage in the shallows, a melee of one on top of the other. Even at this distance, the unnerving clack of legs against shells filled the air.

"Spoiler alert," Nathan said. "Your lures work."

"Just what Larsson deserves," Gianna said.

"Our plan to get them to deep water can still work?"

"Even better, now that there are so many in one place. Get us a head start, I'll turn off those lures, and turn on ours."

"Let's warn Kathy out of the way, and then you throw the switches."

Nathan angled the skiff toward the cabin cruiser. In a minute, they'd closed on the slower boat. Kathy looked at Nathan with surprised relief. He slowed to pace the cabin cruiser on its port side.

"You're alive!" she said.

"It takes more than giant killer crabs and mercenaries to keep a historian down."

"Who's that?" she said looking at Gianna.

"Gianna. Formerly of yesterday's sinking yellow kayak. Presently helping get this crab lure and the rest of the crabs offshore. I'm leaning toward waiving her park entrance fee. Just for today, of course."

"We have just the place to drop the lure. The crabs' den is up ahead. Drop it inside and send them all home. Then we'll seal it shut."

"How?"

"Come around the other side."

Nathan brought the skiff around the *Solitude*'s stern. The propellers from a torpedo hanging from the winch almost hit him in the face.

"Whoa, Kathy. Where'd you get the hardware?"

"A long story. The den's opening should be a half mile dead ahead. Get ahead of us and we'll blast the horn when you're near the location. Lead the crabs, drop the lure, and get out of the way. We'll let the torpedo loose when you're clear."

"You're on. See you after the crab boil."

Nathan gunned the engine, cut across the *Solitude*'s wake, and pulled out ahead of the cruiser.

"That torpedo looks...old," Gianna said. "Your ranger friend knows how to make it work?"

"Totally covered it in class at NPS Orientation. Just another day protecting national treasures."

Gianna didn't smile.

"The owner of the boat knows," Nathan said, more seriously. "Navy veteran. Or Coast Guard. Whatever. We do our part, they do theirs, the world is saved."

"Let's bury some crabs," Gianna said.

CHAPTER 38

The *Solitude* trailed a hundred yards back in the skiff's wake.

"We'd better call those crabs," Nathan said.

Gianna nodded. She tied the lure to the skiff's stern line. She went to the console and switched off the other lures. She reset the controller and engaged their lure. It vibrated and she tossed it over the side. The stern line played out and the lure followed underwater a dozen feet behind the boat.

The mass of crabs crawling over each other in the shallows behind them paused. Then they moved as one in the skiff's direction. And they moved fast.

"It works," Nathan said with false enthusiasm. "Totally awesome. Giant crabs heading our way."

***

"How far out are we?" Kathy called up to Marc.

"Be there in a minute."

"Give them a blast of the horn when you think they're on top of the den." Kathy went back to bailing.

"Your little historian gonna be able to pull this off?"

"He's stayed alive so far. I have faith in him."

Marc compared the den's marking on the map and their location. He held his finger over the button to sound the ship's horn.

***

Nathan looked down in the water behind the skiff.

"The good news is that the lure is working," he said. "The bad news is that the lure is working."

The sea floor below dropped away, but the view remained pretty clear. Giant crabs seemed to cover the sand as far as Nathan could see. And they were closing fast.

Gianna reeled in the lure and held it in the water alongside the boat.

The *Solitude*'s horn sounded.

"That's the signal."

Up ahead loomed a dark hole in the sea floor, partially covered by what looked like a concrete cap.

"I'll never get the lure in there like this," Gianna said. "You'll need to stop the boat so I can drop it in."

"You know that the ocean is full of giant crabs, right?"

"And if this lure doesn't get in the den, it still will be."

Nathan cut the engine to idle and banked the boat into a tight turn near the opening.

Underneath, the crabs caught up. Dozens? Hundreds? Nathan could only guess. They ran into each other, ran over each other, then began to climb on top of each other, creating a crustacean tower stretching up to the lure.

"You need to drop that thing," Nathan said.

"I can't get the rope untied."

One crab scampered up the pile of bodies to the top. It swiped at the skiff with its claw and grazed the hull. The skiff spun sideways. The lure flew from Gianna's hands and dropped overboard.

Rope played out as the lure plummeted straight down and too far from the den. Nathan gunned the engine and wheeled the skiff back toward the opening.

The crab pile disassembled and gave chase. He uncleated the line from the stern and judged the distance from the den opening. He waited two more seconds and let the lure drop.

Momentum carried it forward. Too far forward. It flew over the opening and landed on the concrete cover.

"Dammit," Nathan said.

Then a crab scampered across the pad and accidentally kicked the lure into the den.

"Yes!" Gianna said.

Nathan raised a fist in victory. "Better to be lucky than good."

Crabs fought over each other to funnel down the opening and back into the den. Nathan opened up the engine and headed the skiff back west.

They'd done their part. The rest was up to Kathy.

CHAPTER 39

Marc went back to the torpedo. He unlashed the winch and pushed the fish far enough away to clear the hull. He connected the wires to engage the engine.

Nothing happened.

He tried it again. Nothing. He grounded the positive against the hull. No spark. The battery had died, a connection had gone bad, a relay had failed. He didn't have time to fix whatever had screwed up. He'd have to take the boat in closer, then drop the thing like a bomb and hope that the concussion didn't crush *Solitude*'s compromised hull.

He checked the steering vanes around the props and let out a low curse. They weren't straight. Without power, he couldn't move them, and in this configuration, the torpedo could corkscrew off to anywhere.

That dreaded tightness clamped his chest again. His sinking boat was running out of time. His dying heart was running out of time. There was only one way to make certain this torpedo ended up on target. And he was going to do that alone.

He pulled two life jackets from the starboard storage locker and lashed them together with the rope from the winch.

"What's wrong?" Kathy said from below.

"Battery problem. I need your help. Up here, quick."

She dashed back to him from the cabin. "What do you need?"

"Stand right there." He pointed to the deck around the cockpit's port side.

She stepped up and faced him, looking confused. He shoved the life jackets against her chest. She grabbed them on reflex.

"Gonna need to make this delivery personally," he said. "Now swim."

He shoved her and she fell backward into the water. She broke the surface yards behind the boat and sputtered something unintelligible at him.

The water in the cabin was already two feet deep. He pulled his scuba tank and face mask from below and propped the tank up beside the wheel. With a flick, he turned the BIL PUMP PORT switch off. One of the whining motors in the hull went silent. The boat slowed and the sound of rushing water below became louder. He killed the second pump.

The boat sank lower in the sea. He gave the engine under a minute before it drowned and died. Rising water splashed from the cabin into the cockpit.

The bow dove beneath the waves. The engine coughed and died. All he had left was momentum and prayer. He lined the boat up on the heading for the crab den. Water rose to his knees, then faster to his chest. He donned the facemask, shoved the regulator in his mouth, and opened the tank valves. With a knuckle-whitening grip on the wheel, he braced himself against the rushing water.

The sea swallowed the boat.

Up ahead, he spied an opening in the sea floor where sand had been excavated around the edge of a great concrete cap. The lure's flashing green light blinked from deep within the dark hole. A giant crab scuttled into the opening. A few more were just short of entering. Even if he beat them to it, the concussion ought to blast them to pieces. Just like it would do to him.

Boys of PT 904, he thought, *here comes vengeance.*

He aimed the boat at the entrance. It rolled to starboard from the torpedo's weight, then inverted. The bow jammed into the hole. The torpedo's nose struck the concrete cap.

The sea went white.

CHAPTER 40

"Did the crazy boat owner just push your ranger friend into the water?" Gianna said.

It certainly looked that way to Nathan. Just before the cabin cruiser sank, Kathy had taken an ungainly back-first plunge into the water. Whether she was pushed or fell, she needed to be rescued.

He circled the skiff back to Kathy. Gianna helped her crawl aboard.

As Kathy rolled over the gunwale, a boom thundered from under the sea. The skiff shuddered. Then off the bow, a huge mushroom of white water blasted skyward. Bits of coral, chunks of wooden hull, and shards of crab shell rained down into the water all around them. When the sea settled, a stream of white bubbles marked the location of the resealed crab den.

"The torpedo battery malfunctioned," Kathy said. "The only way to get it on target was to ride it down." Kathy stared at the bubbling water. A lump formed in her throat. "He didn't give me the chance to stop him."

Nathan edged the skiff over to the stream of bubbles. A few larger chunks of the *Solitude* popped to the surface. Suspended sand clouded the water below.

"The opening wasn't that big," Gianna said. "An explosion like that had to seal it."

"I sure hope so," Nathan said. "We're fresh out of torpedoes." He turned to Kathy. "Are you okay?"

She swallowed back the pain of Marc's sacrifice. "Nothing worse than tired, hungry and exhausted."

"Larsson and the rest of his crew are dead. We can head back to Fort Jefferson. Once the red tide scare is debunked, the Park Service will send help or the ferry will return, or both."

"Sounds great." Kathy looked to Gianna. "You were the woman in the kayak? I'm so glad you survived. Can't wait to hear the story of how you did it."

"And you can tell us how you ended up hauling a decrepit torpedo across the Gulf of Mexico," Gianna said.

"And then," Nathan said, "we'll see if anyone else will ever believe either story."

CHAPTER 41

Two days later, Nathan and Kathy sat in full uniform in the office of Deputy Director Cynthia Leister. A map of the National Park system hung on one wall. The emblem of the Department of the Interior hung on the other, alongside an Ansel Adams photograph of Half Dome in Yosemite.

This was the first time they had been alone together since a Navy helicopter had rescued them all from Fort Jefferson. A very relieved Silenius Imports security detail had whisked Gianna away from Key West Naval Air Station as soon as they landed. Then the two rangers had been separated, medically evaluated, and had their statements taken. There hadn't been any formal debriefing, they'd just made written statements. They'd spent that night in separate quarters, awakened to fresh uniforms, and put on a plane to Washington, D.C. None of their drivers, pilots, or escorts professed any knowledge of what was going to happen to them next. The whole post-crab experience had been unnerving.

"I'd say my career is set," Nathan said. "My first week of my first assignment and I get to meet a Deputy Director of the Park Service. Oh, and I got to battle giant crabs."

"You're still planning to write the history of the fort?" Kathy said.

"Only as science fiction."

The door opened and Deputy Director Leister entered. She was in her late-fifties with short silver hair. Her lipstick shined bright red. She looked Kathy and Nathan over as she took a seat behind her desk.

"So, Rangers West and Toland. You've had a hell of a week, haven't you?" She had the gravelly voice of a chronic smoker.

"I guess you could say that," Kathy said.

Leister flipped open a file folder on her desk. She separated out Kathy's and Nathan's original handwritten statements. She sighed.

"So let me get this straight. Under your care, Fort Jefferson and the marine sanctuary around it suffered severe damage. Your explanation is that a rogue CIA agent tried to release giant armored crabs, vintage

1961, so he could send them to the mainland on a killing spree. With the help of a mystery engineer from a secret branch of a small import business, and an eighty-year-old former Coast Guard sailor, you saved the world with an old torpedo."

"When you say it like that," Nathan said, "you make it sound outlandish."

Leister shot Nathan a withering, unappreciative look for his sarcasm. Nathan's smile drooped.

"No one will ever hear this ridiculous story," Leister said.

She gathered up the papers and dropped them in a shredder beside her desk. The motor chugged through the files.

"Here's what really happened," Leister continued. "The park was closed due to a red tide. A recent violent thunderstorm damaged some of the aging fort structure. In an unrelated item, a private firm has donated an old CH-47 to be used as a base for a new coral reef. It's on the east beach awaiting relocation to deeper water. The park will reopen in the near future."

"What about the crab carcasses on Garden Key?" Kathy asked.

"Never saw any."

"And the CIA bunker under the powder magazine?"

"There's no trap door and nothing but sand under the fort."

"And Marc Metcalf's death?"

"Never heard of him. And the Coast Guard has no record of his service."

Kathy stood up, face red with fury. "We almost died, others did, and you think you can just cover all this up?"

"Not *me*," Leister said. "*We* are going to cover it up."

"And why would *we* do that?"

"Because now you're part of a bigger picture."

Leister walked over to the Park Service Map. "Ranger Toland, you're the historian. When was the Park Service founded?"

"On August 25, 1916, an act of Congress created the National Park Service, and President Wilson signed it."

"For the purpose," Leister said, "of regulating, and I quote, 'the use of the Federal areas known as national parks to conserve the scenery and the natural and historic objects and the wildlife therein.'" She rolled her eyes. "Not quite."

Leister stepped over to the shield of the Department of the Interior.

"It really started in 1872, when Congress set aside Yellowstone as a National Park and quickly added other parks over the next few years. All managed under the Department of the Interior. Ostensibly, Congress set them aside for public recreation. But that reason sounds a little hollow. In a time without cars and roads, few visitors could get to any of these places.

"The National Parks are not what they appear. North America was the last and most sparsely populated continent on the planet when Europeans blundered upon it. There was a good reason for that. It was the most perilous. Dangerous creatures beyond explanation lived in certain areas. Contact with mankind always proved to be fatal. Keeping people safe from that was Department of the Interior's job."

"The original department seal," Nathan said, "had an eagle clutching arrows and two crosses. Now I get the symbolism."

"Interior officials presented President Grant with a list of the creatures and their locations. As a military man, he latched onto the idea of creating a network of National Restricted Areas. The secure system would keep the public from the creatures and the supernatural. As a cover story, they were to be called National Parks.

"Thirty years later, the nation's growing population pressed closer to these dangerous locations. There were tragic deaths that had to be covered up. President Wilson wanted tighter control over these threats and created the National Park Service as the cover. Of course, the general population couldn't be made aware of these horrific creatures in their midst. Most were unknown, but some were already local myths."

"Like the Dry Tortugas crabs," Nathan said.

"Exactly. So worried was Wilson about the truth getting out, only one percent of the Park Service employees even knew the real mission. Over time, places of natural beauty without any unnatural threats were added to the system as cover."

"How many of the parks are hot spots like Fort Jefferson?" Kathy asked.

Leister walked back to the map. "We don't know. During World War II, most of the leaders of that secret section were recruited into the OSS."

"The forerunner of the CIA," Nathan said.

"And none of them survived the war. They also took the location of the secret park records with them to their graves. Even today, I'm one of the few people who know anything about the true mission of the Park Service, and I know little more than I'm telling you now."

"And why are you telling us at all?" Kathy said.

"Fort Jefferson isn't the first place where things once quiet have gotten out of hand. Something is affecting these creatures. Rising global temperatures, chemicals in the environment, who knows. But we need to hold the line on these things now, defend against them.

"The two of you handled yourselves well. I want you to work for me, keeping the nation safe from the dangers these parks were founded to contain."

"We would work here in Washington?" Nathan said.

"No, your involvement with me will be completely off-the-books. I'll get you normal assignments within parks that appear to have a problem. I'll notify you when something seems to be going sideways. But there will be no official involvement, no footprints that lead back to Park Service headquarters. If the truth of the park system got out, the first reaction would be overreaction, overwhelming military force that would destroy the parks, along with the threats within."

"And since we're clueless on which parks harbor the dangers," Nathan said, "the government would obliterate them all."

"The public would demand it," Leister said. "Communication with me and support on any mission will be limited. Your priority will be keeping this all a secret, protecting human life, and protecting the parks, and pretty much in that order. You'll never know exactly what you'll be up against, and if you do it right, no one will ever know anything you've done. Are you up for the challenge?"

Nathan and Kathy looked at each other. Nathan tried and failed to suppress a grin. "Uncovering unknown history about the parks? Being a secret agent in a campaign hat? I'm totally up for it if you are."

Kathy paused. "I joined the Park Service to keep all these places safe for future generations, the way other rangers have done before me. It sounds like these creatures could be the greatest threat the parks have ever seen. I'm in."

Leister smiled. "That's what I was counting on. This is the last time we will ever meet. Any communications you get from me in the future will under the name of Vincent Moreno."

"We'll return to Fort Jefferson and await further instruction," Kathy said.

"There's a lot of strange going on out there. I'm afraid you won't have to wait long."

THE END

AFTERWORD

I once read that an author is permitted one suspension of disbelief per story, one bizarre lie he can ask the reader to swallow whole. Then the rest of it has to make sense.

In this story, I played the disbelief card as giant crabs. The rest is pretty accurate.

And even the crabs are just scaled-up versions of ones you see scampering along the beach at low tide. They can live out of water for as long as their gills stay wet. They can survive the loss of a limb. Amp up their shells by a factor of thirty, and they might be bulletproof. One difference from real life is that they hunt by smell, not by sound like sharks and some other sea predators. But having Larsson deploy a series of stinky lures to get crabs to the mainland was too comical to be terrifying.

Coconut crabs are a scary precedent. The crabs can grow up to over three feet wide and weigh as much as nine pounds. The force in their claws is the equivalent of a crushing six tons and they can live up to sixty years. Biologist Charles Darwin reported their claws cracking coconuts. Humans need tools to crack walnuts.

Now on to what's real in the story.

Fort Jefferson is a real place in Dry Tortugas National Park. You can take a ferry from Key West to visit for the day. The general descriptions of the fort and Garden Key are accurate. This book was my excuse to visit there to make sure. Rangers do live there full-time, but it takes more than two to keep the place in the fantastic shape it is in.

Almost all the stories of the fort that Nathan relays are true. The description of the fort's founding and history through the 19th century are correct. The first doctor was Joseph Basset Holder, a scientist more than doctor, who stayed on through the Civil War at this post and ended up working at the American Museum of Natural History. However, while Dr. Samuel Mudd really was an inmate there, he never mentioned giant crabs to anyone.

After the Civil War, frequent hurricanes and yellow fever epidemics convinced the War Department to remove the garrison, leaving a small caretaker force for the armaments and ammunition in 1874. In 1889, the Army turned the fort over to the Marine Hospital Service to be operated as a quarantine station. The U.S. Navy used Garden Key as a coaling station. During World War I, the lighthouse there was decommissioned, but a wireless station and naval seaplane facility was operational.

On January 4, 1935, President Franklin D. Roosevelt designated the area as Fort Jefferson National Monument. On October 26, 1992, Fort Jefferson and the Dry Tortugas were established as a National Park.

The battleship *USS Maine* did stop there before sailing to its doom in Havana Harbor. There were a series of inquests around the explosion that sank her there. None bring up the theory of a stowaway giant crab. See how a credible conspiracy can be spun on the backbone of actual facts? Now let's talk about a second gunman in Dealey Plaza.

PT boats were a real thing, an inexpensive, expedient way to get torpedoes on target in World War II. President, then Lieutenant, John F. Kennedy commanded PT 109 in the Pacific, where it was run down by a Japanese warship, and he rescued many of his crew. During Navy downsizing after the war, most PT boats were unceremoniously stripped of useful bits, hauled up on beaches, and burned. In a coincidence, after the war ended, PT-796 was used in the Key West/Miami area for experimental purposes. (Crab patrol perhaps?) One of the few remaining PT boats, it is today located at the Battleship Cove Naval Museum in Fall River, Massachusetts. Loads of original PT boat manuals and diagrams are online to get your geek on.

The Mark 45 torpedo onboard PT 904 was a real thing, a wire-guided, nuclear-tipped anti-submarine torpedo. The design was completed in 1960 and 600 were made between 1963 and 1976. Of course, not counting the fictional ones I had the manufacturer make for the CIA just a little ahead of schedule. Before Navy vets start writing me, to work on the internals, you had to break the thing apart, so there really wasn't an access port to get to the wiring. But disassembly would have been impossible aboard the *Solitude*, so, shortcut. The descriptions of how it works are all accurate and if you don't believe me, the original Navy training films on the torpedo are on YouTube.

The Bay of Pigs invasion was a true event. In retrospect, the idea of having an army of emigres reinvade their homeland with obsolete equipment and "secret" U.S. military support seems like the CIA trying for its own version of suspension of disbelief. That fiasco isn't brought up much in the U.S., perhaps because it tarnishes JFK's halo, or maybe because the subsequent well-handled Cuban Missile Crisis was a better, bigger Cuba story. No PT boats were involved in the operation.

Special thanks go out to Beta Readers Extraordinaire Donna Fitzpatrick, Deborah deAlteriis, Janet Guy, Paul Siluch, Teresa Robeson, and Belinda Whitney for making Version 2.0 so much better than Version 1.0.

Go visit your national parks. These jewels inspire wonder at every turn. I promise there are no giant crabs.

-Russell James
January, 2019

CHECK OUT OTHER GREAT DEEP SEA THRILLERS

SHARK: INFESTED WATERS
by P.K. Hawkins

For Simon, the trip was supposed to be a once in a lifetime gift: a journey to the Amazon River Basin, the land that he had dreamed about visiting since he was a child. His enthusiasm for the trip may be tempered by the poor conditions of the boat and their captain leading the tour, but most of the tourists think they can look the other way on it. Except things go wrong quickly. After a horrific accident, Simon and the other tourists find themselves trapped on a tiny island in the middle of the river. It's the rainy season, and the river is rising. The island is surrounded by hungry bull sharks that won't let them swim away. And worst of all, the sharks might not be the only blood-thirsty killers among them. It was supposed to be the trip of a lifetime. Instead, they'll be lucky if they make it out with their lives at all.

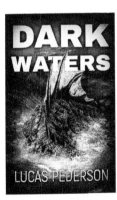

DARK WATERS
by Lucas Pederson

Jörmungandr is an ancient Norse sea monster. Thought to be purely a myth until a battleship is torn a part by one.

With his brother on that ship, former Navy Seal and deep-sea diver, Miles Raine, sets out on a personal vendetta against the creature and hopefully save his brother. Bringing with him his old Seal team, the Dagger Points, they embark on a mission that might very well be their last.

But what happens when the hunters become the hunted and the dark waters reveal more than a monster?

CHECK OUT OTHER GREAT DEEP SEA THRILLERS

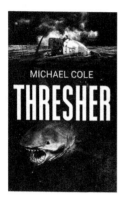

THRESHER
by Michael Cole

In the aftermath of a hurricane, a series of strange events plague the coastal waters off Florida. People go into the water and never return. Corpses of killer whales drift ashore, ravaged from enormous bite marks. A fishing trawler is found adrift, with a mysterious gash in its hull.

Transferred to the coastal town of Merit, police officer Leonard Riker uncovers the horrible reality of an enormous Thresher shark lurking off the coast. Forty feet in length, it has taken a territorial claim to the waters near the town harbor. Armed with three-inch teeth, a scythe-like caudal fin, and unmatched aggression, the beast seeks to kill anything sharing the waters.

THE GUILLOTINE
by Lucas Pederson

1,000 feet under the surface, Prehistoric Anthropologist, Ash Barrington, and his team are in the midst of a great archeological dig at the bottom of Lake Superior where they find a treasure trove of bones. Bones of dinosaurs that aren't supposed to be in this particular region. In their underwater facility, Infinity Moon, Ash and his team soon discover a series of underground tunnels. Upon exploring, they accidentally open an ice pocket, thawing the prehistoric creature trapped inside. Soon they are being attacked, the facility falling apart around them, by what Ash knows is a dunkleosteus and all those bones were from its prey. Now...Ash and his team are the prey and the creature will stop at nothing to get to them.

CHECK OUT OTHER GREAT
DEEP SEA THRILLERS

THE BREACH
by Edward J. McFadden III

A Category 4 hurricane punched a quarter mile hole in Fire Island, exposing the Great South Bay to the ferocity of the Atlantic Ocean, and the current pulled something terrible through the new breach. A monstrosity of the past mixed with the present has been disturbed and it's found its way into the sheltered waters of Long Island's southern sea.

Nate Tanner lives in Stones Throw, Long Island. A disgraced SCPD detective lieutenant put out to pasture in the marine division because of his Navy background and experience with aquatic crime scenes, Tanner is assigned to hunt the creeper in the bay. But he and his team soon discover they're the ones being hunted.

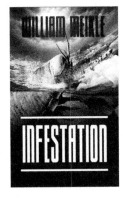

INFESTATION
by William Meikle

It was supposed to be a simple mission. A suspected Russian spy boat is in trouble in Canadian waters. Investigate and report are the orders.

But when Captain John Banks and his squad arrive, it is to find an empty vessel, and a scene of bloody mayhem.

Soon they are in a fight for their lives, for there are things in the icy seas off Baffin Island, scuttling, hungry things with a taste for human flesh.

They are swarming. And they are growing.

"Scotland's best Horror writer" - Ginger Nuts of Horror

"The premier storyteller of our time." - Famous Monsters of Filmland

Printed in Great Britain
by Amazon

33580939R00091